WINNING
THE
CHANAKYA
WAY

Virender Kapoor is a thinker, an educationist, and an inspirational guru. An alumnus of IIT Bombay and the former director of a prestigious management institute under the Symbiosis umbrella, he also holds a Master's in International Relations and Strategic Studies from Pune University. His books on emotional intelligence, leadership, and self-help have been translated into several regional and foreign languages. A prolific writer, he regularly contributes to *The Times of India*, *The Economic Times*, Rediff.com, and several management magazines. To know more about him, log on to www.virenderkapoor. com or mail him at virenderkapoor21@yahoo.com

Other books in the series:

Speaking: The Modi Way
Leadership: The Gandhi Way
Innovation: The Einstein Way
Excellence: The Amitabh Bachchan Way
Succeeding: The Akshay Kumar Way

WINNING
THE
CHANAKYA
WAY

VIRENDER KAPOOR

RUPA

Published by
Rupa Publications India Pvt. Ltd 2019
7/16, Ansari Road, Daryaganj
New Delhi 110002

Sales Centres:

Allahabad Bengaluru Chennai
Hyderabad Jaipur Kathmandu
Kolkata Mumbai

ISBN: 978-93-5333-588-5

First impression 2019

10 9 8 7 6 5 4 3 2 1

CONTENTS

PREFACE

Why This Book?

Most of us have heard of Chanakya and believe that he was a very sharp and intelligent historical figure. Several books have commemorated, rightly so, the wisdom he shared over his lifetime. The focus of most such books has been to show the learning from Chanakya's wisdom, especially for those in leadership and corporate roles. Two of his seminal works—the *Arthashastra* and *Chanakya Neeti*—composed between 350–275 BCE, have been the basic reference material for most authors writing about him.

When I decided to write a book on such a great personality, I had to first decide the aim of this book—will it be another book on leadership or will it deal with strategy?

However, I decided to move away from both leadership and corporate strategy and write something that a common man could put to use in daily life. This book, hence, should help you in enhancing and sharpening your life skills, which ultimately is the aim of this book.

Chanakya's knowledge is vast and could be used in many different ways. Thus, the basic idea was to cull certain nuggets of wisdom from the treasure trove and explain them in such a way that makes the lessons relatable so that one can easily implement them to improve one's life.

This book is about success, achieving success. Whatever is your field of work, whatever you want to achieve—this book will not only set you on the right path but will also be like your lifetime companion. It is based on the wisdom, experience and teachings of Chanakya which have stood the test of time for more than 2,000 years.

It is more fundamental and looks at success which can be achieved by addressing some very basic human traits, behaviours and beliefs. It moulds you inside out and helps you make some basic personality and behavioural changes which will be applicable to any profession that you choose to pursue. This book delves deep into not only the practicality of the idea of achieving but also the philosophy of success.

Winning the Chanakya Way is, therefore, about individual success and how to get the maximum bang for the buck in any given situation. These are those pearls of wisdom which can be applied by every individual to lead a better, more meaningful and worthwhile life. This book largely draws its essence from the relevant sutras in *Chanakya Neeti*.

The Book in Brief

I have touched upon those areas which would be of interest to everyone. Each one of us is trying to move through this maze called life; this book will just show you how to do it as smoothly as possible.

We all want to succeed, and Chanakya will tell you how to be successful in real terms in the chapter titled 'Success'. The chapters titled 'Interpersonal Skills' and 'Self' deal with the aspects of applied emotional intelligence and would tell you, in intricate detail, how to handle others as well as ourselves.

This book will also tell you what the power of character, wisdom and common sense is, which, if truth be told, is very uncommon nowadays. In the chapter 'Saam Daam Dand Bhed', I tell the readers how to put all your might behind something that you want to achieve, using all the tricks of the trade. Featuring Chanakya's most known strategy, the chapter enumerates how to use every trick up your sleeve to attain your goal. Ultimately, *jo jeeta wohi sikandar* (he who wins is the king).

I also address those situations when things go wrong and nothing helps at all. This relates to the concepts of Karma, Destiny and Fate and how, often times, it is impossible to decipher the ways of gods. In those scenarios, how does one accept fate, how does one act or react under these difficult circumstances? I have devoted a full chapter titled 'Destiny' to explore this aspect of life.

Explained: Chanakya's Character and Wisdom

Born in 4th century BCE, Chanakya belonged to the 'Golden Thought Age'; an era which saw greats like Aristotle, Plato and Socrates.

He is generally considered to be a thinker, a teacher and an advisor to the royals, and was also known as the 'kingmaker'. His teachings, at that time, were so basic that they continue to be relevant. He was also known as Kautilya and Vishnugupta.

His contribution to governance was through *Arthashastra* which discusses monetary and fiscal policies, welfare, international relations and war strategies in detail. For living a happy, productive and meaningful life, he wrote *Neeti Shastra* ('neeti' means policy) which is also known as *Chanakya Neeti*. This is in direct relation to the Indian way of life. *Neeti Shastra* is the deliverance of wisdom through pithy and short sentences or verses, referred to as 'sutras'. These aphoristic collections, sometimes known as wisdom literature, have a lot to say and live by.

Out of the 455 sutras in *Chanakya Neeti*, more than 200 refer to *Raajneeti* (the dos and don'ts of running a kingdom or politics). Apparently, Chanakya used these sutras to groom Chandragupta and other selected disciples in the art of ruling a kingdom. Simply put, it is a policy document—a manual of governance and living life appropriately—created and crafted by Chanakya.

Chanakya was a professor of political science, economics and other related areas at the Taxila University. He moved out of this role of a teacher into a bigger role with greater responsibility as a mentor to the kings of those times. He was the one who brought Chandragupta Maurya to power and taught him to rule with élan and pride.

Chanakya was very forthright and in-your-face and always called a spade a spade. Sometimes, someone would call his statements politically incorrect; yet, he was actually right.

It must be noted that in contemporary politics also, teachers have donned the role of a mentor, advisor and a policymaker to the presidents and the prime ministers. Henry Kissinger, for instance, was a professor of international affairs at Harvard and later joined the US administration as the secretary of state—a most powerful and influential position in US policymaking. Robert McNamara who was the secretary of state to John F. Kennedy during the Cold War period, and who evolved several concepts of nuclear warfare, had also served as a teacher at Harvard. Condoleezza Rice, a specialist on the Soviet Union, served as the secretary of state to George W. Bush. Earlier, she was an assistant professor of political science at Stanford University. She was promoted to associate professor in 1987, a post she held until 1993. Dr A.P.J. Abdul Kalam, a teacher and a scientist, was appointed as the scientific advisor to the government of India. Chanakya had performed this coveted role, of a teacher-turned-political advisor, 2,500 years ago.

And now, I would like to look at Chanakya as he stands amongst his great contemporaries and as a first amongst equals. Let us start by examining that in the first chapter.

Virender Kapoor

1

FIRST AMONGST EQUALS: CHANAKYA IN THE GOLDEN THOUGHT AGE

'The unexamined life is not worth living.'

—Socrates

Somehow I feel that on the global arena, Chanakya should have got a better deal in terms of visibility and fame in comparison to other great thinkers of his time such as Aristotle and Socrates. One of the major reasons could be that since the Greek philosophers influenced the West, which later developed much faster than the rest of the world, they got more traction. Another reason could be that after independence, we forgot our own heritage and, therefore, the works of our great thinkers got lost even though their contributions were immense. In this chapter, I will show you a brief glimpse of the time Chanakya occupied in history and highlight that the contributions of Chanakya were in no way less than the other great thinkers of his time. In fact, he was first amongst his equals and needs to be on the world map.

During Chanakya's time, our society had just begun to get organized. New rules were being created and a lot of great minds were working towards this effort across the world. Greece, China and India were the lands where a lot of ideas, in terms of evolution of our society, were being churned out. The focus was on religion, philosophy, war and survival of a nation. The idea of a nation state and nation first emerged during those days, and Chanakya was a pioneer of such ideas.

Science versus Philosophy

If one takes a macro view of human development, one would notice that scientific discoveries came in much after the development of subjects such as philosophy, strategic thought, political science, governance, economics and even the art of deceit. These subjects started evolving more than 3,000 years ago.

Thousands of years ago, day-to-day complex human problems were addressed effectively and judiciously by the thinkers of those days. These thinkers influenced every soul on earth regardless of their race or the colour of their skin. They professed universal truths, which appealed to the whole world. This was philosophy in action. This was the golden thought age.

If today, we live in the age of knowledgeable society, 2,000–3,000 years ago our civilization was dominated by wisdom. Knowledge continuously changes but wisdom is preserved and is eternal. If reading a story is knowledge, then understanding the moral of the story is wisdom. Knowledge can be stored in thousands of gigabytes of data, but wisdom— the essence of it all—can be found in only a few words.

Religion and Warfare

There were a few glorious centuries of golden thought (500–300 BCE) which perhaps created monumental wisdom for humanity to move on. Different religious philosophies also developed centuries ago; they appealed to the masses because they were derived through spiritual thought. Isn't it amazing that the teachings of gurus or founders of faiths went so far and wide even when there were no means of communication—no postal services, no telephones, no radio broadcasts, no internet and no TV! I would attribute the spreading of religious philosophies, despite all the handicaps of distance and time, to the power and purity of those thoughts and the power of their wisdom. They were, therefore, unstoppable.

Concurrently, the art of warfare was also being developed. Religion and war, though always on the crossroads, were the fundamental requirement of mankind; good and bad have always coexisted. Two of the great stalwarts, one in the field of religious philosophy and the other in the strategy of warfare, were born 2,500 years ago—Gautama Buddha at Lumbini, now in Nepal, in 566 BCE, and Sun Tzu in 544 BCE at Qi in China.

While Buddha talked of equanimous mind, meditation and nirvana in India around 500 BCE, Sun Tzu laid the foundation of strategic thought in warfare and statecraft around the same time in China.

'We are shaped by our thoughts; we become what we think. When the mind is pure, joy follows like a shadow that never leaves.'

—*Buddha*

Philosophy and Life

The word philosophy has its origins in the Greek word 'philosophía', which means 'the love of wisdom'. It is the study of knowledge or 'thinking about thinking'. Although its breadth cannot be captured in a few words, I would like to share a few definitions and interpretations here.

Philosophical questions, unlike those of the sciences, are usually foundational and abstract in nature. Philosophy is practised and studied primarily through reflection and does not tend to rely on experiment. It may carry the sense of unproductive or frivolous musings, but, over the centuries, it has produced some of the most important original thought; its contribution to politics, sociology, science and literature is outstanding.

Sample two of the most illustrative definitions of philosophy given as under:

American Heritage Dictionary defines philosophy as the 'investigation of the nature, causes or principles of reality, knowledge or values, based on logical reasoning rather than empirical methods.'

Penguin English Dictionary describes it as the 'study of the ultimate nature of existence, reality, knowledge and goodness, as discoverable by human reasoning.'

Aristotle, the greatest of the Greek philosophers of his time, talked of anger management and human behaviour around 300 BCE in Greece.

During this time, the Greek philosophers were moving towards the radical idea that there were no gods who controlled the destiny of life on earth from some detached mountaintop. Rather, it was man himself who, thanks to his own brainpower and hard work, could decipher the laws of the universe to become master of all nature.

Greek philosophy covers an expansive range of topics including political philosophy, ethics, metaphysics, ontology (the study of the nature of being, existence, life, etc.), logic, biology, rhetoric and aesthetics (the branch of philosophy which deals with art, beauty and taste). Greek philosophy is known for its undeniable influence on Western thought.

Although there have been several Greek philosophers over the centuries, Socrates, Plato and Aristotle are the big three names in Greek philosophy, which is why I will discuss them briefly.

Socrates, one of the first great philosophers of Greece, lived through 470–399 BCE and came up with many original ideas. His most favourite student and another great thinker, Plato, lived through 437–347 BCE. Aristotle (384–322 BCE) was a student of Plato, who started his own philosophical school when he was fifty years old. Although he lived only for ten more years, Aristotle produced nearly 1,000 books and pamphlets, only a few of which have survived. He was known as a peripatetic philosopher, because he lectured his student while taking a walk. Aristotle is considered supreme among thinkers. The scope of his works is truly immense, covering everything from speculations on the nature of the human soul to the physics of the universe; from city politics and personal ethics to the history of plants and animals; from public speaking and poetry to music, memory and logic.

The ideas of all these men from the East as well as the West resound across the world even today with an ever more deafening echo. Man, it appears, had started thinking critically, collectively and simultaneously across the continents more than 2,500 years ago.

Chanakya also belonged to this philosophically productive golden era. His vast wisdom was put to use by the then king, Chandragupta Maurya, to not only run his empire effectively but also to expand it. Chanakya was the teacher of Chandragupta Maurya almost at the same time when Aristotle was teaching the Greek emperor, Alexander the Great.

Alexander the Great invaded the Indian subcontinent in 326 BCE. His offensive upon the land's patchwork of small Hindu empires proved to be highly successful due to the disunity of the petty rulers. Then, it was Chanakya who, feeling deeply distressed, started searching for an able leader. His search ended with Chandragupta Maurya who was highly intelligent, courageous and physically powerful. However, he was a commoner and not blue-blooded. A man of acute discretion, Chanakya only desired to exalt a man of extraordinary capabilities as the king of Magadha so that the offensive launched by the Greeks could be repressed. Kings of the neighbouring states also rallied under Chandragupta's leadership and the last of the Greeks headed by Alexander's former general, Seleucus, were defeated.

Chanakya's teachings, ideas and principles are so basic that they will be relevant at all times. One could draw a parallel with Sun Tzu who wrote the classic *The Art of War* more than 2,500 years ago. The book was about warfare strategy and discussed broad eternal truths concerning military and political philosophy. Again, his knowledge and strategies were so basic and fundamental in nature that most modern weapons are still based on his teachings and observations. Even though the cavalry has been replaced with fast-moving, all-powerful tanks, and spears with machine guns and rocket launchers, his teachings are still relevant because he deals with the fundamentals of human behaviour, broad strategic thinking and politics of war, which will never change. Generals in war rooms as well as in corporate boardrooms are still using his teachings gainfully. Diplomacy, strategy and international relations still remain fundamental in nature; only the lexicon might have changed according to the context and with time. These are like Newton's three laws of motion which will never change and form the fundamental base of classical and quantum mechanics.

Chanakya also demonstrated an appetite towards various areas of human excellence, which probably nobody from his era possessed, especially in the Asian continent. Chanakya's work can be interpreted in different ways—philosophically, politically, technically and, most importantly, practically.

'I must study politics and war that my sons may have liberty to study mathematics and philosophy.'

—*John Adams*

2

PHILOSOPHY OF SUCCESS

'A man is born alone and dies alone; and he experiences the good and bad consequences of his karma alone; and he goes alone to hell or the Supreme abode.'

—Chanakya

Most self-help books on success discuss how to become successful quickly and lay out a format of actions, processes and ideas which you need to follow to become successful. They focus on either corporate success, success in terms of monetary gains or climbing the corporate ladder faster and without much pain.

Literature on success hovers around how to become successful, and seldom discusses what 'success' is. For most people, success is about building wealth, having the perfect life partner, a fancy car, a million dollar business or amassing a huge social media following. These definitions seem to be ego-driven and relate to a person's sense of self-esteem and self-importance; in fact, success, as seen by most, reeks of ego. While it is important to have a positive self-esteem, often it becomes bloated. Consider ego to be pepper, Tabasco sauce or a bit of tadka (spice) in life—too much and it becomes inedible. Therefore, ego is important in a little measure to keep us happy and ticking.

Whenever I asked my incoming MBA batch whether they wanted to be like Amitabh Bachchan or Ambani—the former has more fame and the latter more money—I would always get mixed responses. While in some batches, the ratio would be 7:3, in others it would be 3:7. Once some students said that it is better to be a film star who has huge fame (ego) and sufficient money to live his life well, and I realized that this was logical as well. You need to look for success in a manner that not only satisfies your ego but also makes you live a comfortable life. This is certainly not a formula, but it does make some sense.

Success is in your mind and it is never static. It varies from person to person. Abraham Maslow's hierarchy of human needs fits into this concept very well. (See figure below.)

According to the American psychologist's motivational theory, human needs can be shown in a five-tier model where the bottom ones need to be filled before the higher ones can be attended to. These are, from the bottom up, physiological, safety, love and belonging, esteem and self-actualization. After the basic needs of roti, kapda (clothing) and makaan (housing) are met, a person then longs for esteem, or izzat, and a feeling of accomplishment. At the top of the pyramid is self-actualization, which makes man explore and exploit his full potential and creative abilities to reach a state of contentment and bliss.

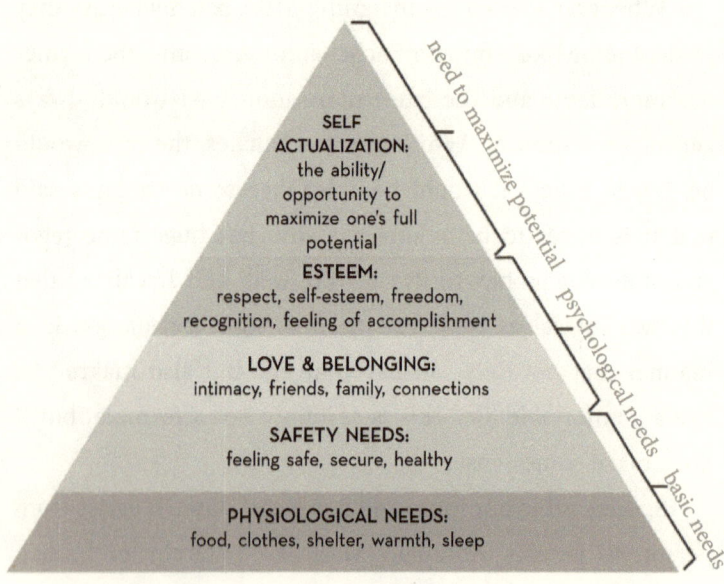

This hierarchy perfectly defines success as a progressive serial movement of human needs. This also tells us that human needs change with time; aspirations progress from survival to satisfaction and happiness.

But, won't it be better if you are at the bottom of the pyramid, and you are clear what you want to achieve or want to be when you reach the fifth level; or better yet, can you achieve all these in smaller bits, not in the serial order as defined by Maslow but in a parallel mode? This is doable, provided you understand what success is and what you are looking for.

If you ask a dozen people about their definition of success, most will say being successful in life is closely associated with having a lot of money. This group defines success purely based on material accomplishments. Others define success through the level of power and control they can exert over others. Everyone has his/her own interpretation of success and he/she has a right to his/her definitions.

Still, most of us have absolutely no clue how we can accomplish success. Do we even understand what it means to be truly 'successful'? Or are we simply repeating the definition of success that society has planted in our mind?

No matter how we look at success, one fact clearly emerges which can't be denied—the sense of accomplishment is extraordinarily empowering. Whenever you achieve whatever you had set out to achieve, you get a great kick. It enriches your perception of life; to be more precise, your perception of the importance of the role you play in life.

'It is better to die than to preserve this life by incurring disgrace. The loss of life causes but a moment's grief, but disgrace brings grief every day of one's life.'

—*Chanakya*

The bottom line is—success is what it means to you and not to the world.

Chanakya Neeti contains pithy sutras, as defined by Chanakya, which are practical, pragmatic, sometimes even bitter and politically incorrect! But, so is life. For instance, is it correct to say everything is fair in love and war to justify actions which may not be right according to others?

Before we discuss the sutras, let us look at a few definitions of success as provided by thinkers, scholars, statesmen, management gurus et al. Surprisingly, 90 per cent of the quotes on success talk about how to achieve success and only a few reflect on what is 'success'.

Sample some of these quotes and see if they match your

definition of success. Do they make life meaningful? Do they satisfy you as of now?

1. 'The singular difference between success and true success is those who achieved true success did not pursue success, they were driven by it. They were those who followed their strengths [...] they were those who lived a highly simple and effective life.' —Sesan Kareem

2. 'Too many people measure how successful they are by how much money they make or the people that they associate with. In my opinion, true success should be measured by how happy you are.' —Richard Branson

3. 'Twenty years from now you will be more disappointed by the things that you didn't do than by the ones you did do. So throw off the bowlines [...] Catch the trade winds in your sails. Explore. Dream. Discover.' —Mark Twain

4. 'Take up one idea. Make that one idea your life—think of it, dream of it, live on that idea. Let the brain, muscles, nerves, every part of your body, be full of that idea, and just leave every other idea alone. This is the way to success.' —Swami Vivekananda

5. 'Try not to become a person of success, but rather try to become a person of value.' —Albert Einstein

6. 'Success usually comes to those who are too busy to be

looking for it.' —Henry David Thoreau

7. 'The only way to do great work is to love what you do. If you haven't found it yet, keep looking. Don't settle.' — Steve Jobs

These quotes may help you find what you are looking for because ultimately you have to be satisfied with what you wish to choose.

Some people find that helping others brings them the joy they are longing for, and therefore, success, to them, looks like a life given to others. Some realize that building a business or product brings them happiness. Some prefer to remain cut off from the world and stay on a mountaintop, and others prefer constant activity.

The simple yet profound truth is that what makes me happy doesn't make someone else happy, and vice versa. My vision of success probably looks nothing like yours, and that's how it should be. Try to answer some specific questions that might help you find your definition of success:

- What truly matters to me?
- What are the things that I am passionate about?
- What do I want to make of my life?
- What lifestyle do I want to live?
- Who do I want to be?

- What do I want people to say about me after I die?

Your answers have to be specific, precise and true to your conscience. Don't generalize by saying 'I want to be the wealthiest person or the fittest person on earth'. Only then will you get to the real definition of your success.

Afterwards, you can even convert that definition of success into your own two-line quote!

The following paragraph by Bessie Anderson Stanley is my favourite and says it all:

He has achieved success who has lived well, laughed
often, and loved much;
Who has enjoyed the trust of pure women,
the respect of intelligent men and the love of
little children;
Who has filled his niche and accomplished his task;
Who has never lacked appreciation of Earth's beauty
or failed to express it;
Who has left the world better than he found it,
Whether an improved poppy,
a perfect poem, or a rescued soul;
Who has always looked for the best in others and
given them the best he had;

Whose life was an inspiration;

Whose memory a benediction.

There is another saying in Hindi, which is also probably the shortest blessing—'*Sadaa khush raho*', which means, always remain happy.

Having defined success for you as of now, let us move onto the nuggets which will make us stronger, clear-headed, motivated, pragmatic and practical individuals in order to become successful.

Some of the sutras sound outrageous while some are practical to the core; some of them even appear to be ruthless, full of deceit and cunningness, but that is how life is. It is up to your interpretation of right and wrong that would help you pick up those which you are comfortable with and shun those that you feel are not according to your temperament and beliefs. A word of caution—keep all of them in mind because even if you are fair to others, it is not necessary that others would be always fair to you.

In the following chapters I discuss that to be successful, it is important for you to know how to deal with others as well as how to deal with yourself. I discuss the importance of education, knowledge and how to acquire these and apply them prudently in your life. The power of character is equally important for success, and life becomes meaningless without it. Wisdom and common sense are two sides of the same coin and if you have these on your side, life is a cakewalk. Self-actualization is something that is a must-have for a successful satisfied life. The last but not the least important factor is the power of destiny, faith and the power and might of the Almighty, which keeps you grounded all the time.

Through the intellectual and pragmatic prism of Chanakya's sutras, this book covers all that is required to lead a successful, meaningful and happy life.

'Before you start some work, always ask yourself three questions—why am I doing it, what the results might be and will I be successful. Only when you think deeply and find satisfactory answers to these questions, go ahead.'

—*Chanakya*

In a Nutshell: What is Success?

1. **Meaning of Success**: Success means different things to different people. Do we even understand what it truly

means to be 'successful'? Or are we simply repeating the definition of success that the society has planted in our mind?

2. **Success is Subjective:** In order to understand what success means to you, you must look at the fundamentals of success, which can be achieved by addressing some very basic human traits, behaviours and beliefs.

3. **Your View is Not *the* View:** The simple yet profound truth is that what makes me happy doesn't make someone else happy, and vice versa. My vision of success probably looks nothing like yours, and that's how it should be. The bottom line is—think what success means to you and not what it means to the world.

4. **Accomplishments Are Empowering:** No matter how one looks at success, one cannot deny that a sense of accomplishment can be extraordinarily empowering. When you achieve whatever you had set out to achieve, it enriches your perception of the importance of the role you play in life.

5. **Be Happy:** The ultimate aim of life is to remain happy. What is the point of being successful, whichever way you define success, if you are not happy? As mentioned earlier, *sadaa khush raho*. This should be the ultimate definition of success.

3

INTERPERSONAL SKILLS

'Managing people is not rocket science; it's even more complicated because you are dealing with people, and no two are alike.'

—Dr Samir Kapoor, former head, Recruitment,
Standard Chartered Bank

Dealing with people is the most challenging, yet essential task for every human being. We need to interact with friends, family, colleagues and even with our enemies. This is all a part of the game as they say. Some people have a natural flair, talent, or ability to deal with others effectively and they, therefore, can manage to handle situations and relationships extremely well on a day-to-day basis. They are, in a way, gifted and intelligent. This ability is formally recognized as emotional intelligence and is the most prominent part of human excellence. Even though it is considered a 'soft' skill, a life skill, it is crucial to survive and thrive.

Many leaders and professionals from all walks of life fail because they do not know how to handle relationships. They simply can't deal with people the way one should. Those who do, get far ahead of their peers and competitors. Every human being is different in nature and has a unique mental makeup which is as distinctive as his/her fingerprint.

My personal experience tells me that dealing with people is not a science, but an art; it's a talent, a stroke of genius which some possess, and others, who do not have this ability, envy. Even if one doesn't have this 'intelligence' as god's gift, with concerted and conscious effort, one can develop this as a skill.

No wonder, then, that, over the centuries, many great philosophers and thinkers had their opinions, with regard to dealing with people, expressed in the pithiest of manners.

Chanakya was one of these great thinkers who had a deep understanding of human behaviour and therefore one can draw some very effective and relevant ideas about dealing with people from his ideas.

What can we learn from this great thinker of yesteryear whose ideas are still relevant, maybe more than before? Let us see Chanakya's wise advice on managing people.

Types of People

Before one learns how to deal with people, it is essential to understand them and their basic characteristics first. Chanakya provides interesting insights into the types of people:

1. **A True Friend**

    Ature vyasane prapte durbhikshe shatru-sankate.
    Rajdware smasane cha yah tisthati sa bandhawa.

    It means that the person who is with you at the time of festivities, in distress, in a crisis caused by enemy attack, in the royal courts and in the crematorium, is your real friend.

    Simply put—a friend in need is a friend indeed. However, in the present age of social media and mass communication, we call everyone our friend. But, is it right? These 'friends' agree, disagree or argue with you on some serious and many silly issues. Most of them have never met you, nor are they going to meet you in future. The definition of a friend, according to the dictionary, is 'a person with whom one has a bond of mutual affection, typically one exclusive of sexual or family relations'. Practically speaking, a friend should be dependable, someone you can trust and someone who will stand by you when you are facing a crisis. He/she is with you through thick and thin—whether you are ruling or you are in the dock. Most of us have a few close friends; one should focus on them. With regard to friends, quality definitely matters more than quantity. It is always advisable to have a few friends who will stand with you at any time you need them. And you must reciprocate when they need you.

Nowadays, when joint families have become a matter of the past and nuclear families have also got busy with their day-to-day work, friends have emerged as the biggest support system in an emergency. Thus, it is worth building a close dependable bond with a few people in your city, place of residence or workplace. These people will not only wish you on your birthday but will also be ready to take you to the doctor if required, even in the dead of the night. When you have a few close friends, help is always just a call away. Identifying such friends is an art; one should not get carried away by sweet talk and nice posts on Facebook or WhatsApp—these really don't matter, what matters is solid personal support.

2. **Humble and Decent**

Aho svit vichitraani charitaani mahaattmanaam.

Laxammem trinaaya mannyante taddbharen namanti cha.

Being humble is one of the great qualities which one must look for in their close dependable friends. According to Chanakya, people who respect richness and laurels, yet are grounded and humble are the ones worthy of counting as friends. Arrogant friends, especially those who have an ego because of their riches, should have no place in your friends' list. The moment you come to know of this trait, you should break that friendship because such friendships, even when forged consciously, do not last long. Many of us get swayed by people who have swanky cars and big residential mansions, as well as great clothes to flaunt their wealth. This should also not happen.

3. **Devilish Minds**

Attyantlepah katutaa cha vaanee, daridrataa cha svajaneshu vairam.

Neech prasangah kuleenseva, chinnhaani dehe narkasthikaanaam.

People with bitter speech and sharp tongue, people with bad temper and those with spite and hatred for one's own relations should be considered bad company. Those who believe that weaker people are their slaves and treat them with disrespect are also not worthy of friendship. There are people who treat caretakers such as drivers, cooks and maids unfairly. They use impolite language and don't consider them as fellow human beings. If they can't respect others, then how can they respect you?

Here is an incident that will bring out this aspect very clearly. Once, a girl and a very rich man, who were to get married, went to a restaurant for dinner. They both ordered what they wanted to eat and the waiter served them the dishes. One of the items was not hot enough and the man got very annoyed. He started shouting at the waiter, abusing him and saying that 'people like you need to be taught a lesson; you are from a poor background and know nothing about good manners'. The waiter was almost on the verge of crying. The girl was upset with this behaviour of her would-be husband. On the way back, she told him, 'If you treat someone who is lower in stature than you badly, it reflects on your character'. Real-time behaviour-monitoring is a big input to a person's character.

4. **Wicked People Who Can Be Dangerous and Poisonous**
   Takshasya visham dante makshikaayaa mukhe visham.
   Vrishchikasya visham puche sarvaange durjane visham.

Chanakya, in his own poetic way, said that poison is close to the teeth of a snake, in the head of a fly or a bee and in the tail of a scorpion, but a wicked person has poison in his entire body. He meant that a wicked person can be much more dangerous than all these poisonous reptiles and insects put together.

This is real wisdom and has a lot of depth. You can save yourself from a scorpion, but a person with a poisonous mind can harm you to the extent of wiping you out. A villain can make your life miserable; with his cunning, he can destroy your reputation, your wealth and your health too. Chanakya advised one to keep away from such people. Although it is a difficult thing to find out who is your well-wisher, there are always ways to identify them. Here are some general examples to learn from. I have seen partnerships going for a toss and some ending up in a legal battle because of a wrong business partner. A wicked person may seem nice and innocent but when he decides to hit you hard—that being his hidden intention—he can be very dangerous, and the whole experience could be disastrous and painful. Remember, it is very difficult, if not impossible, to prejudge someone's intentions (niyat). One should always do a reference check from former employers even while employing a driver or a help at home.

In the era of entrepreneurship, one has to be very careful in selecting a partner because a new business venture takes time to set up. If one partner gets greedy and the other partners are not careful and alert, he can milk the system right from the beginning. In such cases, stakes are very high and one must check from several sources about the character and characteristics of a partner before getting into an alliance. In a marriage also, both sides try to do some due diligence. Things may still go wrong, but if due diligence is done, chances of things going wrong are reduced to a large extent.

Here is a story of two men whose rise and fall I personally witnessed:

Two young men started a business venture. Since one of them was strong in finance and the other was good in marketing, they divided their work and responsibilities accordingly. The marketing arm started functioning well, but the finance person started spending lavishly and without due diligence. He bought goods at higher price points. He didn't apply his mind towards bargaining, and instead of a multi-vendor approach, he leaned on one vendor who supplied products at a higher price than the market price. Gradually, he started taking a commission or a cut from the inflated price. The partner, who was looking after the marketing arm, trusted the other partner and never bothered to cross-check the accounts. Slowly, the company went into losses; however, the finance guy made money from these kickbacks while the marketing guy lost all his investment. If he had kept a tab on the finances and hadn't trusted his partner blindly, this could have been avoided.

This does not mean you should not trust your partner, but the bottom line is, don't trust blindly, and keep a close track of finances and workload.

5. **Wicked Nature**

Na durjanah saadhudashaamupaiti,
bhautprakaarairapi shikshyamaanah.
Aamoolasiktam payassa ghriten,
na nimbavrikshoh madhurattvameti.

Bad nature is hardwired into a person as if in his DNA. Therefore, the above sutra means that no teaching and no amount of effort can turn a wicked man/woman into a good-hearted person and one must deal with him/her accordingly. To give an example, he further stated that no amount of milk and ghee given to a neem tree can turn its fruit sweet. Like bitterness is neem's 'fitrat' (inherent nature), wicked nature is one's fitrat which cannot be changed.

One has indeed witnessed people changing their attitudes, but those are very few. In actuality, a person who has a wicked and poisonous mind is very difficult to change, whatever means you may adopt. There is also a saying in Hindi—*Chor chori se jaye, hera pheri se na jaye*—which roughly translates into 'a thief may stop committing thefts but he will not stop conning people'.

Chanakya also said that one should not give a second chance to a crooked person, especially in a battle or war, where it is a question of life and death. In fact, Chanakya and his mentee Chandragupta Maurya were dealing with a situation of life and death as they were trying to establish a new kingdom. For them, it was a question of survival of the fittest as well as of the cleverest. Chanakya was forging alliances with other smaller kingdoms to come together so that they could defeat and overthrow the Nanda Empire under King Dhana Nanda. Chanakya learnt a bitter lesson the hard way over the years and thus, always prescribed ruthless action. He experienced deceit, back-stabbing and double-crossing by other kings and their advisors over the years. This is exactly what happens in the game of thrones and politics. As they say in Hindi, '*Doodh ka jala chhach ko bhi phook phook kar peeta hai*'—once bitten, twice shy. Even though I cannot give any specific incident which taught him this lesson, his overall experience and learning led him to believe in this philosophy regarding human nature.

There is a famous story of how Prithviraj Chauhan spared Muhammad Ghori's life but lost his own eyes once Ghori defeated him, as he was a wicked man. Their story is an example of how one should not let their heart rule their head while dealing with a wicked enemy:

Prithviraj, the Rajput king, had a big empire in northern India with his capital in modern-day Delhi. He had another capital of his kingdom at Ajmer. Ghori, a Muslim emperor, wanted to conquer parts of India and was ready to wage a war against Prithviraj Chauhan. In the first battle of Taraori, in 1191, Prithviraj Chauhan's cavalry charged and routed the Ghurid (belonging to Ghori) cavalry, capturing Ghori. When Ghori begged for his life, Prithviraj allowed him to go, despite his generals asking him not to do so. Some say it was a Rajput tradition to treat prisoners well, and a repenting prisoner should not be killed. When, the following year, Ghori came again, Prithviraj advanced with his army and sent a letter to Ghori, asking him to return, reminding him of his previous defeat and also of the fact that his life had been spared.

Ghori replied that he was in India on the orders of his brother, Ghiasuddin, and that he could only retreat after he got a word from him. Ghori sent this letter in the evening and also moved his camp back a few kilometres to feign retreat. On receiving his letter and seeing Ghori move back his camp, Prithviraj assumed that Ghori would not attack. Yet, Ghori treacherously attacked in the early morning hours when Prithviraj and his army were sleeping, and was able to win this war.

The worst is that he took Prithvraj as prisoner only to humiliate him in front of his courtiers. When Prithviraj was produced in front of Ghori, he looked straight into Ghori's eyes. The Muslim emperor got very annoyed and asked him to lower his eyes. Prithviraj refused, and Ghori ordered that Prithviraj's eyes be gouged out with burning hot iron rods. It was a painful punishment. Thus, one cannot help but think that if Prithviraj had not spared Ghori in the first war, he could have lived very happily. Therefore, remember this—first assess the person and then take appropriate action.

As a corollary, there is another lesson to be learnt—beware of traitors within. Jaichand Rathod, a Hindu, ruled his kingdom from Kannauj. Due to personal rivalry with Prithviraj, he never joined hands with him. Instead, he secretly helped Ghori to defeat Prithviraj and, with his help,

Ghori managed to defeat Prithviraj in the second Battle of Taraori. Ghori knew that an enemy's enemy is your friend and he used Jaichand to his advantage. Prithviraj, on the other hand, didn't expect Jaichand to act like a traitor. Therefore, Prithviraj made his first mistake by freeing Ghori in the first battle, and in the second battle, he didn't keep a close eye on Jaichand's treacherous activities. The lesson learnt is that if you have someone who has rivalry with you then you must keep a watch on him so that he does not collaborate with your competitor or adversary to take revenge.

'Don't let a thief into your house three times. The first time was enough. The second time was a chance. The third time means you're stupid.'

—*C. JoyBell C.*

Dealing with People

We have seen till now that to understand the nature of people is not easy. Sometimes, in our weaker moments, we make decisions from our heart, that is, we may take a softer approach, which we may regret later. Since the nature of human beings is very complex and not easy to discern, we must first gauge the intentions of the person to deal with him/ her accordingly. These are some of the steps Chanakya has advised to deal with people in various situations:

1. **Identify a Wise Man**

   Prastaavsadrisham vaakkyam prabhaavsadrisham priyam.
   Aatmashaktisamam kopam yo jaanaati sa panditah.

   It is very important to keep good people with you because company matters. Chanakya said that a person who talks with reference to the context influences people through logic and expresses love and anger appropriately is a vidwan, or a wise man. Such people know when and where to speak, and they display affection and wrath in a measured manner according to the situation. These people must be respected, and their inputs and suggestions must be regarded and considered.

   When one watches TV debates today, one is surprised that the panellists keep beating around the bush and seldom remain focused on the topic. They dodge the anchor's questions and even the viewers get exasperated and irritated with such panellists. However, there are some panellists who are articulate and to the point; viewers appreciate their contribution as they believe that they talk sense.

2. **Cheerful and Intelligent People Bring Cheer and Duffers Bring Grief**

Moorkhashishyopadeshen dushtastreebharanen cha.
Dukhitaih samprayogen panditoappyavaseedati.

Chanakya clearly elaborated the difference between a wise and a cheerful person and a duffer and a foolish person. He said that teaching a duffer or a foolish student brings grief upon the teachers too. Anyone who has been a teacher would know that to have an intelligent student is indeed a pleasure. Even when you give a talk at a college or a corporate gathering, you expect a responsive, participative and intelligent audience. My experience tells me that whenever I deliver a talk at any corporate event and the audience is not energetic enough, my morale as a speaker goes down. Similarly, associating yourself with a sad, depressed and brooding person will make you feel sad. Therefore, one must keep the company of cheerful and bubbly people. They spread good vibes and an atmosphere of positivity.

Emperor Akbar kept Birbal as his minister because he was very witty and humorous. He always presented his ideas in the form of a joke, pun or witty remark. Humour requires intelligence. Without intelligence, a person will not even understand a joke, leave aside crack one.

3. **A Sound, Sensible and Loyal Team Is Essential for Winning**
Shrutvantmupdhashud mantrin kuveert.
For a king, it is essential to have wise ministers. Similarly, a prime minister (PM) must have cabinet ministers who are wise, open-minded and have unflinching loyalty to the PM. Without a wise cabinet, it is difficult for a PM to function properly. That is why coalition governments don't function very well, as the PM loses his freedom to take proper decisions which sometimes may not be very popular with the public.

4. **One Wheel Cannot Run the Chariot**
Neink Chakra Paribhrampati.
Here again, Chanakya laid emphasis on teamwork because a leader, a king or a PM cannot work alone. The cabinet and the PM are two wheels of a chariot and must work in sync to achieve the ultimate objective which the king has decided.

4a. **Weigh All Options Before Arriving at a Decision**

Mani pratimaninmatmani dwitiya mantramutyapadyet.

Here he said that a leader must weigh all pros and cons of a problem in his mind before taking his decision.

5. **Never Make a Strongheaded Person Your Close Confidant**

Avneet snehmatren na mantrey kuveert.

No matter how dear a person is to you, if he/she is headstrong, don't make him/her your advisor and never your close confidant, who would come to know all your secrets. Such people may spill the beans and even your closest secrets when they decide to.

6. **Success in a Project Is Possible If Discussions Are Kept Secret**

Mantrakhane karyasidhibharwati.

For example, you are launching a new product; then, before the launch, a lot of planning, designing and production activity has to take place. This is open to industrial espionage and exploitation by your competition. Therefore, everything related to this project must be shared only on a 'need to know' basis and only with a minimum number of people, who are directly involved with the project. This strategy is more important in government functioning where the surprise element is essential. If some new tax regime is being brought, then the facts and figures have to be kept secret till it is officially declared.

7. **Beware of the Sweet Tongue**
   Padutare trishnaparey sulabhmatisandhanam.
   Here Chanakya showed his brilliance by telling us a very critical trick of the trade which people apply to appease others. He warned people, saying that if someone is very sweet for no apparent reason, then something is not right. You may have noticed that an innocent child also behaves very well in front of his parents if he wants a raise in pocket money or a favourite toy or permission to go and stay with a friend. However, adults are likely to deceive you with their sweet talk too. Wrong business deals are cut when people come under the spell of a sweet-tongued person. Political goof-ups at the international level also take place just because one head of the state has charmed the other!
   This is also called buttering or 'makkhan lagaana'. I use the expression—too sweet for my liking—for such guys. It is good to have a person who tells you your mistakes on your face rather than saying 'three bags full, sir' all the time.

Therefore, the bottom line is that keep such people at an arm's length and don't get impressed by or fall prey to their sweet talk.

'The secret of many a man's success in the world resides in his insight into the moods of men and his tact in dealing with them.'

—*J.G. Holland*

Don't Let out Your Secrets to Even the Closest of Your Family or Friends

It is important to keep your trade secrets and personal secrets with you. Never share these with any one. Even your intentions must be kept close to your heart. Don't let people know whom you trust and whom you don't.

1. **Keep Your Distance**

   Vallabhasya karkatwamdharam yuktam.

   This is something very important as a leader or a person heading an organization. I have noticed this about the modern generation that people become too familiar with teammates. According to a saying within the armed forces, 'Be friendly but never familiar.' If you become too close, you become, as I call it, 'too close for comfort.' If you are on backslapping terms with everyone, then a time will come when people will start taking you for granted and may not even listen to you. Another saying within the forces is, 'A senior should forget that he is a senior but a junior should never forget that he is a junior.'

Unfortunately, today, with too much liberty and growing consciousness towards establishing friendships, this is being forgotten. A senior tries to become friendly, but a junior tries to be familiar. The moment you become familiar or allow people to take liberties with you, you are treading on dangerous ground. Once that thin red line is crossed, you can't redraw it.

2. **Keep Your Secrets**
Kshataknaard bhidhdhutay mantra.

Chanakya said that a secret is no more a secret if it reaches six ears—that is three people's ears. A state secret must remain between the king and the concerned minister. If it is shared with someone else, it can—and it most probably will—get into the open. When three people know it, then you don't even know who leaked it. In today's environment where information is power, it is very important to guard vital information. Unfortunately, almost all our data is on computers which can be hacked. Therefore, much is being invested to build cybersecurity by almost every country.

Secrecy and deception go hand in hand. During the Second World War, the British intelligence got hold of two encryption machines developed by the Germans called 'Enigma'. This development was of such strategic importance that Winston Churchill, the then PM of England, ensured that it was classified as 'Ultra Secret', that is, beyond top secret. These machines were used effectively by the British to intercept the German military high command's messages. It is also said that they turned the tide in favour of the Allied forces and were a major cause for the defeat of the Germans.

This 'plan' worked only because of the utmost secrecy about these machines. In intelligence parlance, there is a term—on a need-to-know basis—which means a plan should be divulged in as much detail as is required at that level.

In 1976, a raid at Entebbe Airport in Uganda by Israel was another classic example of politico-military secrecy. An Air France airplane was hijacked by Palestinian terrorists who wanted the release of prisoners in Israel and four other countries. No one knew what was being planned except the PM, few people in the cabinet and the top military leader. The troops were briefed about their task on the aircraft! As a result, President Idi Amin of Uganda didn't know what hit him. He came to know only after the job was done by the Israeli soldiers. They just lost one man, Lt Col Yonatan Netanyahu, commander of the task force, and got all the hostages back safely.

This principle of maintaining secrecy is required to protect patents, inventions, innovations and new medical and medicinal research. If followed properly, one can even save a company from industrial espionage.

3. **Punish Judiciously**

Yatahrh dandkari syat.

Chanakya believed that while dispensing punishment, one should neither be too harsh nor too lenient. A harsh punishment might not go down well with the teammates and people might start disliking the team leader. But, being too lenient is also not good because then there is no fear of the law or rules. How much is too much is an important judgement call and one must analyze the context of the situation, which comes with experience. That is why dealing with people is not a science, it is an art.

4. **Treat People Well**

Sanukrosh bhartramajivet.

Chanakya professed that if you treat people well, they will respect you and you will truly deserve their service. This holds true for your subordinates, your peers and even people who work for your personal comfort like drivers, cooks or your household help.

5. **A Lazy Person Cannot Take Work Out of Others**

Na bhootyan preshyati.

This is Chanakya's best mantra for entrepreneurs. If you are lazy, people under you will never work hard. In order to make them work, you ought to be on your feet as well. This is applicable at every level. If a CEO is not hard-working and sincere, his senior officers' team will automatically become lethargic. They would simply say, 'If the boss is not interested, then why should we work?' This is basic human nature. Hard-working people know how to take work from their people.

6. **Don't Be Transparent and Keep Your Cards Close to Your Chest**

Susiddhamaushdham dharmam grihachchidram cha maithunam.

Kubhuktam kushrutam chaiva matimanna prakashyet.

Here Chanakya took a different approach to being smart. As they say, 'Transparent does not mean being naked!' One should not hesitate to hide one's silly mistakes. For example, if, by mistake, you had something which is not to be eaten as per your religion, there is no need to advertize it. He also talked about sex and said that one must keep their equation with their spouse or partner secret. What one does with them needs to be cherished in privacy. Shortcomings of your household and your siblings need not be discussed with others.

'A friend is one who has the
same enemies as you have.'

—*Abraham Lincoln*

Dealing with the Enemy

Enemy is a harsh word to use and is usually used in battles where people *have* to kill each other. The modern reader can instead think of an adversary, opponent, rival, antagonist, combatant, challenger or competitor. They may sound a little more civilized but actually they all mean the same. Like with an enemy, you follow the Geneva Convention; similarly, in business, in spite of cut-throat competition, you have to follow business ethics. Chanakya looked at an enemy as the enemy of the state or anyone who was against national interest. Yet, his ideas and methods on how to deal with the enemy apply equally well in modern times.

1. **Enemy's Enemy Is Your Friend**

   Ekantrint mitramshyate.

   This is an age-old saying in international relations and diplomacy, and is equally true at a personal level. One must identify the reverse too—enemy's friend can be your enemy. It works both ways. Right from gang wars to battles between countries and wars between blocks of nations, this aspect is always relevant and plays a crucial role in dealing with others appropriately. It is also important in our day-to-day affairs to understand who will stand by us and who will not, depending upon our equations with others.

   The Second World War was full of such equations which determined the balance of power and how the war progressed. Hitler befriended Russia in the early years but, as soon as he started winning on the western front, he cast it aside. He had only used Russia's might to scare the rest of Europe, which looked at Russia as their arch enemy. This friendship with Russia was only to make it an enemy of the other European nations.

2. **Don't Trust Anyone Fully, Even Your Closest Ally**
   Sandhyayaiyevekto wa.

   This is the height of wisdom and a cunning mind. As per Chanakya, national interest is of paramount interest; the nation state always comes first. Thus, it is judicious to not trust anyone fully regarding matters of the state. This is a perfectly safe and sane hypothesis. This saying is also true for individual people. Even though cheating and deceit are tricks as old as time, they have become, of late, very common as we have become greedier than before. Again, this sutra is applicable to almost everyone—you cannot trust your domestic help fully, you cannot trust your subordinate fully, you cannot even trust your boss completely. You may trust a person, but you shouldn't share everything with him/her. It does sound overcautious, but it is true.

   Chanakya said that even if you have a treaty or a pact with the neighbouring country, you must still monitor your enemy's activities and intentions. Never take your enemy for granted.

For instance, the German-Russian non-aggression pact was signed on 23 August 1939, just before the start of the Second World War. It is a classic example of deceit under a contract amongst nations. Also known as the Molotov-Ribbentrop Pact, it was a neutrality pact between Nazi Germany and Russia. Hitler had cleverly kept Russia—a military power to reckon with—at bay as he invaded the rest of Europe. Without Russia getting involved, he had a clear run-up to the English Channel. On 22 June 1941, within two years of signing the pact, Germany declared war against Russia by launching the biggest land attack across 2,900 miles of Russia's border, called Operation Barbarossa. Stalin was ignorant till the last minute even as preparations were under way for such a massive operation. Stalin did not take his intelligence inputs regarding this build-up seriously; in fact, he brushed them aside as mere overreaction.

Back home, the Panchsheel Pact was signed between China and India on 29 April 1954 under which both the countries agreed to mutual non-aggressive, peaceful coexistence and non-interference. Jawaharlal Nehru and his defence minister, Krishna Menon, were both caught unaware as China attacked India on 20 October 1962. There are umpteen such examples of breach of contract and, therefore, one has to be careful of such violations.

3. **Never Disclose Your Weakness**
   Atmachiddra na prakashayet.
   Chanakya said that you should never divulge your weakness to your subordinates as well as your enemy. In fact, never tell your frailties to anyone. This is a golden rule because the moment people know your weakness, they can exploit you. The same should be applied while dealing with an enemy—keep your cards close to your chest; no one should know what your next move will be. Try to be unpredictable, to a reasonable extent.

4. **Keep Your Enemy Deceived**
   Yavchatroshidhradra tawad budhstein va skandhein va baham.
   Chanakya advised to keep your enemy in the dark even if it meant employing artificial or deceptive behaviour. The idea is to keep your intentions closely guarded till you find out his/her weakness. *Shatruchidre prahreit*—once you know the weakness, attack on the it with all your might.

Diplomacy

"Diplomacy is the art of letting
someone else have your way."

—*Sir David Frost*

Tact or diplomacy go hand in hand. This can make you win a war without even fighting it. Diplomacy is one of the most important methodologies to deal with a political adversary, a business competitor, a nasty friend and most importantly, in handling international relations. That is why foreign ministry officers are known as diplomats. Chanakya developed refined methods of diplomacy during his times which he practised as well as preached through his sutras. Here are some very important ones.

1. **Be Nice to the Person Whom You Seek Favours From**
   Yasmaacha priyamichcet tassya broo yaa priyam, vyagho mrigvadham gantu reetam gayati suswaram.
   Chanakya said that you need to be extremely polite to the person from whom you need a favour. In fact, in a sly way, he suggested to not divulge your intentions, if you have any, against that person. This may sound unethical, but that's

what diplomacy is. Chanakya gave the example of animals who try to woo their prey into a killing area by making mellifluous sounds. Diplomacy is all about niceties.

'Diplomacy is the art of telling people to go to hell in such a way that they ask for directions.'

—*Winston Churchill*

---

2. **Focus on the Larger Interest**

Raja veshya yamashchaannih chaurah paalakyaachakaah pardukham, najaananti ashtamograamakatakah.

Chanakya said that in every profession one has to focus on the larger interest and, to a large extent, self-interest. When you do something within your professional duty, you cannot please or satisfy everyone. If you attempt to do this, you will never be able to do your job. For instance, when a policy is made by the head of the state, there will be some who will be happy and some who will not be happy. Similarly, a prostitute doesn't worry about her customer's problems; she just cares for the money provided, in exchange for her services. If a doctor gets emotionally attached to every patient, then he himself will fall sick due to depression.

Therefore, one has to focus on the larger picture when dealing in professional matters. And, as long as you are doing things with good intentions, do not worry about a few who may be dissatisfied. You can't be nice to all the people all the time.

3. **Deal with People According to Their Strengths**

   Anulomen balinam pratilomen durjanam.

   Atmatullyambalam shatrum vinayen balen vaa.

   You must deal with your adversary or enemy or even competitor appropriately, according to their strengths and weaknesses. When dealing with a powerful enemy, try to win him over by offering favours. With a wicked and cunning one, try to stay away, and with an enemy of equal strength, be aggressive or submissive, according to the situation.

   Chanakya went on to say that if you confront a person who is more powerful than you are, head-on, then you are going to end up with a definite defeat. Keep him in good humour and even confused by not divulging your true intentions. If an enemy is wicked and shrewd, you might not know his intentions or what he is upto. In such a case, try to avoid him as much as possible, but keep trying to find his weak spots and hit him at an appropriate opportunity. In boxing too, if your opponent is stronger, you look for favours by giving him opportunities to hit you and make him feel exhausted, and then, at an opportune time, you hit hard to knock him out. If the guy is as good as you, you can attack and defend as you do in a normal game.

Hit Hard When You Need to Hit

1. **Deal with the Wicked Enemy Ruthlessly**
   Hastee hastasahastren shathasten vajinah.
   Shringani dashahasten deshtyaggenn durjanah.
   Chanakya proposed that the only way to deal with a bad person is to crush him/her completely or go away from him/her. Never be lenient or soft towards your enemy.

2. **As Far As Possible Stay Away from the Enemy**
   Khalaanaam kantakaanaam cha davi dhaiv pratikriyaa.
   Upanamukhbango vaadorataive visarjanam.
   Chanakya said that never stay in the land of the enemy territory as you are always vulnerable. He gave examples and said that one should keep a distance of 1,000 hands between an elephant and himself, 100 hands between a horse and himself and a full country between himself and

a wicked enemy. He accorded the highest level of threat to a clever enemy.

3. Keep Your Enemy Under Control

Hastee tvamkushmaatrena baajee hasten taapate.
Shrnghal khuhasten durjanah.

As an elephant is kept under control with a goad and a horse by reins and a cane, similarly, a wicked person must be dealt with no mercy and handled with a strong hand. In Hindi, there is a saying—*Laaton ke bhoot, baaton se nahin mantey*—which translates to 'people who need a stick, don't listen to your pleadings and appeals'.

4. Act Harsh with a Harsh Enemy

Krite pratokritim kurryaat hinsen pratihinsanam.
Tatra dosho na patati dushte daushtyam samaan charet.

If the enemy is harsh, you be equally harsh with him. If he is ruthless, you also be as ruthless as or even more ruthless than the enemy.

'Never hit if you can help it, but when you have to, hit hard. Never hit soft. You'll never get any thanks for hitting soft.'

—*Theodore Roosevelt*

Temper and Tongue

1. **Control Your Tongue**

   Yaddeechchasi vasheekartu jagadeken karmana.

   Parrapavaadashaassttreebhyo gaam charanteem nivaarya.

   Chanakya said that you can overpower the whole world by just one action, and thus, you must put a restraint on your tongue while criticizing someone. This is important, as the moment you talk ill of someone, it goes out into the public domain and is bound to reach the person concerned, sometime or the other. This, in turn, hurts your credibility and dependability. It breaks friendships and creates a rift between people.

2. **Controlling Anger**

   Krodho vaivastavo raajaa trishnaa vattarni naadee.

   Viddyaa kamadudhaadhenu santasho naandaanaam vanam.

   It goes without saying that anger can be your biggest bane in life. Chanakya said that dealing with different people may invoke different feelings—sometimes happiness, sometimes dismay and sometimes anger. Thus, keeping your cool and remaining composed is a great art worth practising.

3. **Beware of Arrogance**

Nastyahankar sameh shatru.

Arrogance is that one trait which makes a person unpopular with everyone. Being humble and grounded gets you friends. Humility attracts people towards you while arrogance and ego repel even your friends. Whether you are successful or otherwise, it is always advisable to remain level-headed and never present yourself as conceited or haughty.

Arrogance and ego can bring destruction and devastation to your career as well as to your friendships, which matter so much in life. Your peers at work will not tolerate you if you always impose your ideas on them and try to show that you are the best and no one is better than you.

Being Human

Some of the sutras of Chanakya sound too straightforward; many times, his advice is to be ruthless with people depending upon who you are dealing with and in what kind of situation. One may be familiar with expressions like 'personal battles', 'corporate wars' or 'perform or perish'—all these reflect a cold-hearted or unsparing attitude towards people in your journey towards success.

However, Chanakya also looks at the softer side of human nature and has enough to say in this regard as well:

1. **Be Kind to Elders**

   Vinayasya mool vridhyopseva.

   You learn the meaning of humility when you serve the elderly, when you respect the elderly. Unfortunately, this is on the decline as people have become more and more materialistic; they are running in a never-ending rat race, the elders at home forgotten. This responsibility is being passed on to the state and the government. There are discounts and advantages given to senior citizens in terms of interest rates, concessions on travel and preferential treatment in waiting areas, etc. But, at an individual level, we all must be respectful and helpful to elders. You are not successful if you earn millions and your parents are living in discomfort, without receiving your love and longing for it all the time. Elders require your company and your time more than your money.

2. **Show Mercy to All**

   Vaacha cha maansa shauchmindriyanigrah.
   Sarvabhotadtaya shauchmetachaucham parnmarthinam.

   The greatest duty of a human being is to be human

and keep one's thoughts and speech as well as actions pure in terms of caring for others. Everyone must do good to others and show mercy to the ones who may have committed a mistake. Once again, it is important to understand that while chasing success and victory, one should always keep their humane side intact. Look at companies like Tata, Wockhardt, Microsoft, Bharati, etc.—their promoters have done a lot for humanity as a company and also as individuals. They have helped thousands in finding a better life.

'Blessed are the merciful,
for they will be shown mercy.'

—*Jesus Christ*

Worldly-wise

One needs to be worldly-wise to earn respect and make people look up to you.

Chanakya has some very straightforward ideas which have a deeper meaning for our relationships:

1. **Anything in Excess Is Not Good**

   Atiroopen vai seetaa chaatigraven raavanah.

   Atiddanaad balirbadddho hayati sarvatra varjayet.

   Chanakya said that excess of good as well as bad is not desirable. Ravan got killed because of his excessive ego and the feeling that he was invincible. People who are extra charitable may also get into trouble as they may give their entire wealth to someone they love and end up as paupers. He mentioned Bali Maharaja as an example from Hindu mythology who gave a gift of three paces of land to Lord Vishnu, and because of this charity, he lost all the three worlds. If you are not careful and too kind-hearted, you may be duped.

   I have another incident to share. Once, I was going with my wife in our car to pick up a friend from the airport in Delhi. It was June, and Delhi was sizzling at 45 degrees. I stopped the car at a traffic light. A poor old woman approached me and said, 'My daughter is in labour and she needs help. Can you take her to the hospital?' I told her that I was getting late, but she could take her daughter in a taxi and gave her ₹300 as I could see a young girl clutching her stomach lying on the footpath and could gauge the seriousness of the situation. The old woman also wanted water and my wife gave her a flask full of cold water and asked her to keep that flask as she may need it.

In the evening, when we shared this incident with our friends, we were told that this was a racket and we had been duped!

2. **Stay Away from Trouble and Natural Disasters**

   Upasargeannyachakre cha durbhikshe cha bhayaavahe.
   Asaddhujansamparke plaayati sa jeevati.

   It is always better to move out immediately from places of natural calamities like volcanic eruptions, floods, droughts or jungle fires. Don't wait for it to hurt you or before it's too late. This is also applicable to riots and fights like gang wars as you can be caught in the crossfire. This is also a matter of judgement and it may be better to err on the cautious side than repent.

   During the partition of our country, the situation was very unpredictable, as Hindu-Muslim riots had started. Many got killed; families got butchered. Those who left the problem areas in time could save themselves.

3. **Punishment Should Be a Deterrent**

   Amitro dandmityamayat.

   The existence of an enemy depends upon the policy of the punishment. If you do not have a credible deterrence, people will not take you seriously. In Singapore, the punishment for possessing drugs is death. As a result, they have been very successful in stopping the drug menace. The nation that possesses a nuclear weapon considers itself safe from invasion because the enemy cannot take a chance with such a nation. Credible deterrence means that you have a bomb and you will use it if pushed to a wall. Similarly, any policy you make in the organization, at the national level or even at home for the kids must invoke a bit of fear and deterrence. Therefore, if the cost of the crime is raised, people will obey.

4. **Progress Is in Your Hands**

Atmayatto vridhivinaashi.

If you decide to work hard and succeed, no one can stop you. But, if you are hell-bent on destroying yourself, then no one can help you. Many people don't listen to a friend's, parent's or counsellor's advice and later repent.

5. **Use the Penal Code with Discretion**

Dando hi vigyane praniyatey.

A penal code is not to be applied as 'one size fits all'; that is why only judges give judgement in a court of law. A judge applies his mind to the type of crime, the background of the accused and the circumstances of the case before deciding on the punishment. Discretion is very important and must be applied judiciously. Therefore, a crime conducted under one section of the penal code carries a defined band of punishment, for example, imprisonment for three to ten years. The quantum of punishment depends on the above factors and what the judge feels about it.

6. **Never Dishonour a Weak King**

   Durbalopti raja navmantavya.

   Here Chanakya referred to the respect of the institution and the chair. He said that one should never insult a chair or a high office even if it is held by a weak person because, ultimately, he/she is not demeaning a person but the institution. For example, the Supreme Court is the last resort for justice and the final authority to give legal dispensation. It is the highest authority as per the constitution. Maligning the Chief Justice for political brownie points is incorrect. Such things are against the national interest. Similarly, today, under the garb of freedom of speech, one finds heads of states being ridiculed and sometimes even abused. Remember that the president and the PM are a nation's chief executives.

7. **Don't Let Your Wisdom Get Clouded**

   Shatrumitravat Pratibhati.

   When your wisdom gets clouded or enveloped in a fog, your enemy seems to be your friend. Again, it boils down to having a clear mind and a balanced judgement about people. One should not let it get cluttered by frivolous inputs or by a false front put up by someone. As I always say, wisdom comes with experience. Therefore, I would suggest that young entrepreneurs should always take an elderly person as their mentor and take his/her opinion to avoid getting into a mirage type of situation.

'Knowledge comes from learning,
wisdom comes from living.'

—*Anthony Douglas Williams*

In a Nutshell: Interpersonal Skills

1. **Understanding People:** Dealing with people is the most challenging job and this applies to everyone on this planet. You cannot win in life if you don't win over the people you deal with.

4

DEALING WITH YOURSELF

'God grant me the serenity to accept the things I cannot change, the courage to change the things I can and the wisdom to know the difference.'

—Reinhold Niebuhr

L ife is like a rollercoaster ride. It is immensely important to keep one's wits about oneself and remain positive during all the ups and downs that one has to go through in this journey called life. One should understand what one can achieve and what one cannot. In order to remain relevant and perform well professionally, one has to constantly update their skills and become more mature with time as years pass by. Happiness and grief are a part of life. It's never dark all the time and sunshine also doesn't last forever. One has to weather the storms, rain, thunder and other jolts alongside success and happiness. One should try to remain unnerved in every situation. While money is not everything, it is an important part of life. You should not be too materialistic, but you cannot deny yourself a reasonably good life which is not possible without money. Hence, one needs to manage money well.

Handling your own emotions is another important part of living, especially as life is becoming more and more demanding, competitive and challenging on almost all fronts. How to keep your emotions under check has become crucial, so that they neither trouble you nor do they come in the way of your relations with other people.

In order to be a winner, you must have a personal code of conduct and behave according to that code. This would vary from person to person depending on your value system, circumstances and upbringing. There is also a code of living defined by society and we must align our own definition with that of the society as well as the country in which we live.

Chanakya has given a lot of insight into an individual's appropriate behaviour, how he should project himself and how he should conduct himself in front of others to seek respect and cooperation.

All of his sutras introduced in this chapter are full of

wisdom which can be followed by each one of us to live a successful and happy life.

Self-assessment

Before you assess yourself, it is important to figure out where you stand now.

1. **Importance of Self-knowledge**
   Nasti kamasamo vyadhirnasti mohasamo ripuh.
   Nasti kopasamo vahnirnastijnanatparam sukham.

   Here Chanakya says said that there is nothing more important for your well-being and happiness than self-knowledge. He also said that there is no fire worse than the fire of wrath, whether you give it or receive it.

   He further said that there can be nothing more damaging than uncontrolled desire for sex and infatuation especially, for someone who is not your legit partner. There have been disasters within kingdoms when the kings have eyed women belonging to other kings. Honey traps have often been used in several spy scandals and continue to be used even now. Ministers have had to resign because of such scandals. Bill Clinton, in recent memory, was on the verge of impeachment because of his affair with Monica

Lewinsky. The affair between Cleopatra and Mark Antony is yet another example of love and lust where kingdoms got threatened.

Chanakya also emphasized on the power of knowledge and said that it gives the greatest joy and contentment. If you have wisdom and knowledge, you have conquered the world. You will align your mission and vision according to your capacity, hence will remain happy. Today, we say knowledge is power. Imagine—Chanakya said this more than 2,000 years ago!

Many wonder how people with knowledge become successful, whereas others who don't acquire as much knowledge serve under these people. Cracking competitive exams after hard work and getting into the civil services or a prestigious college is a case in point.

2. **Support System**

Gunam sarvatra tullyoapi seedttyeko niraashrayah.
Anadharyamapi maannikkyam hemaashrayamapekshate.

You may have all the qualities of a winner, yet you will need support to blossom. A virtuous person will also get disheartened and distressed if he/she doesn't get any support. Giving the example of a gem, Chanakya said that it needs to be mounted on a silver or a golden base so that it is truly valued. When planted, a tree sapling also needs the support of some bamboo stick as well as some protection so that it can grow and become self-sufficient. In our day-to-day world, people who have the support of parents and friends are lucky. At work, you need mentors, and in some industries, you need a godfather who can help you climb the ladder. There are only a few people who manage to do well even without a bit of push and help.

3. **SWOT Analysis**

   Kah kalah kani mitrani ko deshah kau vyaya dgamau.
   Kashchdham kd me shaktiriti chityam muhurmuhuh.

   Imagine the wisdom of Chanakya and how far-sighted he was. We talk of SWOT—Strengths, Weaknesses, Opportunities and Threats—in modern management, which has just been in existence for 150 years. Through this sutra, Chanakya said that one has to constantly keep monitoring who one's friend or foe is; how the times are and which way the wind is blowing. Before you sow, you must check what kind of land it is, how much fertility there is and what kind of crop can be yielded, and what would be the expenses, overheads and risks involved. You must check whether you have the capacity to undertake this project or not. Don't bite off more than you can chew. You must examine every aspect, opportunities as well as threats, if you want to come out a winner. He warned that most failures occur because people only look at their strengths and opportunities but miss taking into account the threats and the weaknesses.

This is relevant for small businesses, start-ups as well as established business organizations. This is also applicable at a personal level. For instance, when you plan your child's wedding, you must be realistic enough to understand how much you will be able to sustain in terms of expenditure. Don't overstretch yourself, else you will regret it later.

'Behaviour is the mirror in
which everyone shows their image.'

—*Johann Wolfgang von Goethe*

Personal Behaviour and Conduct

Having understood your strengths and weaknesses and what good habits you should inculcate in order to be a better person, you must thereafter use these while dealing with others. Here are some important tips.

1. **Don't Blow Your Own Trumpet**

   Par-proktaguno yastu nirgunoapi guni bhawet.
   Indroapilaghutdm yati swayam prakhydpitairgunaih.

   Never praise yourself; let others praise you. If others praise even a useless person, he would gain some status. Similarly, if god starts praising his own virtues, he would belittle his/her status. There are people who cannot think beyond themselves. Such people are never liked by others.

2. **Add Value to the Things that You Own**

   Ayiktasvaamino yuktam yuktam neechasya dooshanam.
   Amritam raahave mrittyurisham shanker bhooshanam.

   Chanakya said that a worthless thing acquires value if a great man uses it, and a great thing becomes worthless if a useless person possesses it.

   I always tell my students to add value to the chair they occupy and not to worry about the price of the chair. When a great man like Albert Einstein scribbled his theory of relativity on an ordinary piece of paper, the value of that paper went up a thousand times. Such things are auctioned for millions of dollars. Einstein's violin was auctioned for £373,000 and a letter written by him on the day he renounced his German citizenship, after realizing he could not return due to the rise of the Nazis, was sold at an auction for £22,800. His 'happiness' note, which said, 'A calm and humble life will bring more happiness than the pursuit of success and the constant restlessness that comes with it', written in German, fetched $1.8 million at an auction. Clothes worn by Elvis Presley or Michael Jackson are still a craze and are auctioned at high prices. If you had 5 acres of land, what would you do with it? You could build a great college campus, recruit the best faculty and enrol the best students. The campus could be built with money, but to make it a success, you would need the right quality of teaching staff. In this case, the campus and the buildings are the hardware, while people are the software. People matter, and what they do also matters. You remove the people and bring in 500 buffaloes and you have converted the same building into a ranch.

3. **Stay Away from Fools**

Moorkhastu paribartavyah prattyaksho dvipadah pashuh.
Bhinattih vaakyashoolen adrishyayam kantakam yathaa.

Chanakya warned that one should never keep the company of foolish people. He referred to them as two-legged animals who can hurt you with their words and also get you into trouble. He said that the best people to befriend are those who possess common sense and can solve day-to-day problems. In the stories of Akbar and Birbal you have hundreds of anecdotes where Birbal, with his wit and common sense, was able to give Emperor Akbar simple solutions to complex problems. Advisors and friends must be selected with this criterion in mind.

4. **Keep Your Secrets to Yourself**

Arthanaash manastaapapapam grihnyaashcharitaani cha. Neechamvaakyam chaapamaanam matimaann prakaashyet.
The basic thread of this sutra is that loyalties and friends change with time and, therefore, one should not share personal information with friends who may turn foes tomorrow. He especially warned that one should never share the following with anyone as sharing them will not solve the problem—loss of one's wealth, a personal tragedy or suspicion regarding their partner's character. People will not be able to help you with any of these problems, but later, they could exploit you because they know something which is very close to you and is your weakness.

5. **Keep Your Intentions a Secret**

Manasa chintitam karyam vacha na prakashyet. Mantrena rakshayed gudham karye cha api niyojayet.

Chanakya said that one should never divulge one's plans and what one is going to do next. While implementing your plans also, never indulge in too much fanfare at the time of execution, and immaturely or inadvertently give out information in advance. One should learn to do things quietly.

6. **Handle Your Enemy Tactfully**

Anulomen balinam pratilomen durjanam.
Aatmatullyambalam shatrum vinayen balen vaa.

While dealing with someone who is more powerful than you, you must have a strategy of winning him/her over with favours and gifts because direct confrontation will cause sure defeat. Avoid a wicked enemy because he/she can never be trusted during a fight. Be aggressive or submissive with an enemy whose power matches yours equally, depending upon the situation. This is the essence of diplomacy.

7. **Be Impactful**

Yasmin rushte bhayam naasti tushte naiv dhanaagamah.
Nigrahoanugraho naasti sarushtah kim karishyati.

A person is of no consequence if he/she is unable to give happiness to others because of his/her power, resources or money. Such actions generate respect. Otherwise, what is the point of having resources if they cannot be used for others? Similarly, if a person's wrath and displeasure cannot cause anguish and fear in others, then also he/she is of no consequence.

In a practical scenario, if you have been put in a position of power, then try to help people. Not many are bestowed with such a position. In case you have to impart justice, ensure that your justice or reprimand is such that a person would never make the same mistake again.

8. **Look Stronger Than You Are**

Nirvishenaapi sarpena kartavyaa mahatee phanaa.
Vishamastu na vaappyastu ghataatopo bhayankarah.

Chanakya said that even if a snake is not venomous, it must rise to its full height to frighten people. Your stance matters to the opponent. If you look weak and scared, it will become a morale booster for your enemy or your opponent. In games as well as daily life, it is good to look confident and assertive, which will always go to your advantage.

9. **Do Not Be Lazy**

Na alasya rakshit vivdhartey.

A lazy person cannot grow his assets nor can he/she do well in life. This is true in every aspect of life.

Without hard work and dedication, you can never win. Procrastination, delaying things and not being punctual and dedicated—all these form a part of being lazy.

10. **Implement the Rules That You Make**
Nitishdshtrdnugo raja.
When you make a rule at home or in your workplace, you must ensure that it is followed to the hilt. If this is not done, then you will not be respected and no one will listen to you thereafter. Many of us make rules but then take the attitude of '*sab chalta hai*' (anything works) and let people do things they want to do. This breeds disrespect and disobedience. In our country, this is the biggest problem. All the rules exist as per law, but implementation is poor. That is the reason things don't work as they should.

11. **Dedication Is Most Important**
Upaypoorva na duskar syaat.
If one is determined to find a solution to the problem, then there is no problem that cannot be solved. The best way to succeed is to apply your mind, and take help from others too, so as to get to the bottom of the problem and have a clear-cut plan in front of you. After this, it becomes easy to solve the problem.

12. **Timing Is Also Very Important**

Kalvakti karya sadhyet.

There is a right time for every work or task. The one who knows when to start the work is the winner. In politics, for example, timing matters a lot. You cannot fight elections when public sentiment is not with you. Similarly, there is a concept of 'first-mover advantage'—those who take the first opportunity always win as they have a clear advantage over opponents.

13. **Don't Change the Time Plan**

Kaalatikramaat kaal evam falaya viptee.

Once a time plan has been made, changing it or interfering with this in between can cause failure. During World War II, Hitler had planned to invade Russia in the summer, as Russian winters are very cold and troops might not have been able to survive. For some other military operations in the Balkans, he postponed the dates by a month—from 15 May to 22 June 1941. The rest is history; Germans got caught in the rains followed by the harsh cold weather of Russia, and this turned the tide against Germany, and decided the fate of the war.

14. **Not a Moment Should Be Wasted**

Kshan Prati Kaalvikshepya na kuryatsarv katyeshu.

Here Chanakya talked of urgency and said that not even a moment should be lost while undertaking a task. As the saying goes, '*Kal karey so aaj kar, aaj kare so ab*', which means that instead of doing something tomorrow, do it today; in fact, do it right now. If you lose even a moment in the beginning, you can seldom make up for it in the end.

15. **Handling Natural Disasters Not in Your Hand**

Daiv shantikarmana pratishray davyam.

Never panic because of natural calamities; face them with your chin up. Earthquakes, floods, droughts and volcanic eruptions affect many lives, but those who take this as part and parcel of their life and move on will definitely succeed. In today's context, there can be a personal tragedy, a policy change by the government, which can impact a business, an economic downturn or sudden onslaught of a powerful competitor entering the market, which can upset your personal as well as business plans, but one should try to be calm and composed while dealing with them.

16. **Managing Your Boss**

Swamin sheel gyatwa karya sadhyet.

It is important to understand the nature of your boss before you start working with him/her. This is a tremendously practical and important advice. If you know your boss's mind, then half the problem is solved. Remember, he/she is the boss and you are supposed to assist him/her, help him/her and make his/her work a little easier and not the other way round. Good employees understand the nature and attitude of the boss first and then do their work accordingly. For example, if a boss is a stickler for time and appreciates his staff to be well-dressed, then it will be in your interest to be punctual and properly groomed every day.

17. **Dress Up Appropriately as per Age and Occasion**

Vyochnrup vaish.

Chanakya stated that you must look your age and dress up accordingly. It is so true even today. You shouldn't dress up in party clothes for a business conference or a formal interview. So, whenever you are stepping out, keep in mind—age and occasion matter while choosing your attire.

18. Never Be Ungrateful

Nakritgyasya narkannivartanam.

Chanakya put it very bluntly and said that if you are ungrateful, you have committed the biggest sin for which you should be sent to hell. This is true in modern life as people are more ungrateful than before. Even children, for whom the parents have done so much, become thankless, and some even ill-treat them.

One should be grateful to god for what he has given us and shouldn't cry for what one doesn't have. Be grateful to those friends who helped you during your difficult times. Be grateful to your teachers who taught you and made you a capable person.

If you are ungrateful, people will take you to be egoistic and selfish, and a time may come when no one will help you and you may become isolated.

Emotional Management

Emotional Intelligence (EI) is now recognized as one of the most important attributes of human competence which lets you navigate appropriately through the maze of day-to-day problems while dealing with people and with yourself in different situations. Managing your own mind, mouth, heart and thoughts is very important for your being successful in life. All these come under emotional management. It is a very vast subject, but here I will pick up a few important ideas that Chanakya explained through his sutras.

1. **Determination Is the Greatest Virtue**

    Yaddooram yadduraaraaddhyam yachcha doore vyavasthitam.

    Tattsarva tapasaa saaddhyam tapo hi duratikramam.

    The most difficult task can be accomplished or the most distant dream can be achieved if you are determined to work for it. Perseverance, willpower and determination are very similar in nature and once you decide to do something, whatever be the cost, rest assured the battle is half won. Mountain climbers work hard and train harder to conquer Mount Everest, and they have to make several attempts before they succeed. Civil services aspirants work hard consistently for years and yet often do not make it in the first chance. Those who do not give up and try again are successful in their second or third attempt. Determination and delayed gratification are parts of emotional intelligence, which play an important role in our success.

2. **Power of Discretion**

Aahaarninddraa bhaya maithanaani samaani chaitaani nrinaam pashunaam.

Gyaano naraanaamadhiko vishesho gyaanen heena pashubhih samaanaah.

Humans and animals both have the need for food, sleep, water and sex. Animals also experience fear and danger like humans. However, the main differences between them—the ability to differentiate between what is right and what is wrong—make humans superior to animals. If a person does not have the discretionary power, then he/she is unable to distinguish between good and evil, ignorance and knowledge, right and wrong. If he only indulges in eating, drinking and sex and does nothing else, then he is like any other animal.

Chanakya distinguished between the emotional mind and the rational mind. Fear and the sense of danger are experienced through the emotional mind, while logic and decision-making are controlled by the rational mind. The same thing has been the topic of research in recent years where thinkers and psychologists talk of EI and Intelligence Quotient (IQ), which is the measure of logical intelligence.

3. **Foul Language Is More Potent Than a Burn Which Causes Pain**

Aagnadaahdapi vishishta vakyarushyam.

It is a fact that if you insult someone in public, it can leave a mark on that person for his entire life. For instance, if you step on someone's toes by mistake and say that you are sorry, he will forgive you. But, harsh words and an insult will hurt him more and leave a wound which will not easily heal. Therefore, be very careful in choosing your words while dealing with people. Even a pauper will not accept abusive language. An insulted person is likely to keep that in his/her heart for a very long time and may even seek revenge.

4. **Arrogance Is the Biggest Folly**

Nastyaahankar sanah shatru.

Arrogance is your biggest enemy and has destroyed even the most powerful of people. When you are arrogant and conceited, you treat everyone with contempt. You look down upon your closest allies and advisors and that is the beginning of the end for you. Therefore, whichever high pedestal you are on, never be arrogant or look conceited.

'The nose of the mob is its imagination.
By this at anytime, it can be led.'

—*Edgar Allan Poe*

5. **Mob Mentality**

Gaatanoogitko loko.

A man behaves as the mob behaves or how others behave. People follow a crowd blindly. Those who have the ability to discern between right and wrong are always better off. A short but powerful concept, this has been used by rulers, politicians and generals even centuries after Chanakya said it.

This, in fact, is the basis of propaganda and how Joseph Goebbels, under Hitler, created the propaganda machinery to brainwash the Germans. Adolf Hitler, during World War II, had said, 'The receptivity of the masses is very limited, their intelligence is small, but their power of forgetting is enormous. In consequence of these facts, all effective propaganda must be limited to a very few points and must harp on these in slogans until the last member of the public understands what you want him to understand by your slogan.'

Another thinker, Charles Mackay, had stated the same in explicit words. He had said, 'Men, it has been well said, think in herds; it will be seen that they go mad in herds, while they only recover their senses slowly, one by one.' 'Bhed chaal' is what we call it in Hindi, meaning 'herd mentality'.

The lesson is, one should use their own mind too when one sees most people having a singular opinion.

'To be meek, patient, tactful, modest, honourable, brave, is not to be either manly or womanly; it is to be humane.'

—*Jane Harrison*

Rationale versus Emotions

Chanakya had a lot to say about how the human mind works in two spheres—one is the heart which is associated with emotions and the other is the head that is the rational part of our thinking. One has to intelligently shift between the head and the heart according to the situation, to move smoothly in life. Sometimes, tough decisions have to be taken and you cannot let your emotions (that is, your heart) get the better of you. Similarly, at times, you need to show compassion while dealing with a person or a situation—this is a decision that one should take from the heart. It is surprising that Chanakya talked about these issues a long time ago which are now being studied under Emotional Intelligence. Formal studies regarding EI were conducted just three decades ago. This again demonstrates Chanakya's foresight and wisdom.

1. **Love Mellows Down the Opponent**

   Bandhannaani khalu santi bahoono.

   Premarajjukrotiabandhan mannyat daarubhedanipunoapi shandanghrirniskriyo bhavati pnakajkhoshe.

   Love is a powerful tool which can mellow down people. He gave the example of the black bee, which can penetrate material as hard as wood and yet comfortably gets enclosed into the folds of a lotus flower, which represents love and affection. Similarly, you can tame the most difficult opponent with your good gesture, diplomacy and love.

2. **Do Not Be Callous or too Harsh in Your Behaviour**

   Pramaadad drishita vashmupassyati.

   When you are dealing with your enemy, there is no need

to be brash and show off your strength through your words, body language or demeanour. In films, the hero openly warns a villain that he will come back for him. What is the need of all this rhetoric? One should hit hard, and that too without warning or divulging one's actual intentions.

3. **Be Enthusiastic but Keep Your Wits about You**
   Sahsein na karyasiddhee bharwati.
   In actuality, a person may be brave and full of enthusiasm, but he will not be able to succeed unless he is fully aware of the problem and has a solution in mind. One gets to learn this with experience and sometimes the harder way. The harder way is when you go through several bad experiences due to your unpreparedness which become lessons for life.
   Most young people get into a business or a situation which they have not thought through and later regret their decision. In such a situation, it is better to weigh all the pros and cons before jumping into something. As they say—*josh ke saath hosh bhee zaroori hai*, which means that along with enthusiasm, you need to keep your wits about you as well.

4. **It Is Difficult to Judge the Calibre of a Person**

   Natsatyardha purush ratnasya.

   An individual, like an expensive and most exquisite gem, has several qualities. It is very difficult to evaluate a man, as his qualities may show much later. There are a couple of things to this—do not discard a person based on face value; give him a chance to prove himself.

   You need to spend more time to gauge a person's potential. As the head of a business school, my selection process underwent a change after I realized that written exam scores may not be the most appropriate way to assess a candidate. Therefore, I started giving more weight to personal interviews conducted by a panel of people from the industry and the academia. When you have a one-on-one discussion for a couple of hours, you are close to picking the right candidate.

5. **People Who Have Bad Intentions Always Doubt Others' Intentions**

   Swayamshudh paranshankatey.

   Those who are fraudulent and dishonest always see others as themselves, which may be a problem of their mindset. In India, people do not want to do their job properly and evade taxes, but will always keep finding fault in the system. They will not do anything to improve the system, but will always expect the system to work according to them. Therefore, do your work properly first, fulfil your duties and only then can you point a finger at others.

6. **He Who Criticizes Others Is Inadvertently Pointing out His Own Inefficiency**

Yeh sansadee pardosh shansati sa swadosh prakhyan yati.
Chanakya here referred specifically to a parliament or a court of law. He said that, in public discourse and debates, and everyday discussions also, the focus should be on the flaws of the system and how to improve them; one should not make it personal by criticizing the debater or the opponent. In the Parliament and courts, one should not just criticize people but criticize the policy, or highlight issues with facts and through debates. He who does that lowers the stature of such a discourse or august gathering. In fact, this is what one watches on news channels today. Despite the anchor repeatedly interrupting personal jibes, panellists do make it personal many times, which is in bad taste and lowers the esteem of the panel discussion. Parliaments also witness such noisy behaviour of parliamentarians.

'Don't take life too seriously.
You'll never get out of it alive.'

—*Elbert Hubbard*

Happiness and Grief

Life is full of ups and downs, and success and failure, and one has to learn to live with them. Happiness comes to everyone and so does grief. There is no home where there are no celebrations and also no home where there is no death of a loved one which brings gloom. One must learn to handle success with grace and grief with strength. Chanakya has given his ideas on this aspect of life.

1. **There Are Certain Things in Life that Give Us More Pain than a Body on Fire**
   Kaantaviyog suajanaapmano rinsyashesha kunripasya sevaa. Dariddra bhavo vishya sabhaa cha vinagnimete pradhanti kaayam.

   According to Chanakya, the following scenarios hurt an individual the most—separation from one's beloved, insult by close relatives, when you have lent money to someone and they don't return it, working for a wicked king, poverty and association with bad people; these situations are distressing.

How true this is! Look at crimes being committed by people. The reasons are similar. Someone did not return somebody's money. Someone insulted a person and he was murdered. Love-based crimes are committed if someone snatched somebody's partner away. Like in Ramayana, Ram kills Ravan because he abducted Sita.

2. **Things That Cause Grief**

   Vriddhakaale mrtitaa bhaaryaa bandhuhastagatam dhanam.

   Bhaojanam cha paraadheenam tishrapusaam vidambana.

   Death of a spouse in old age causes great grief and is an irreparable loss. Similarly, if money is under the control of a dominating sibling, it is very demeaning. Obviously, all relatives and siblings are not dominating or mean, but it is important to remember that some might be. If you start dominating your sibling, especially his or her finances, problems are likely to emerge in the family. Also, depending on someone for your food and daily needs causes grief. This is a larger lesson which needs to be understood while dealing with family members, brothers, sisters and parents.

The greatest lesson in today's age is that you must save money to live comfortably. Parents should not give away their savings and property to children as long as they are alive so that they can never be humiliated. Nowadays, people seem to have forgotten these basic values. Children sometimes don't remember what their parents did for them.

Let us examine this further—god has hardwired the emotions of love and sacrifice in parents for their children, especially mothers, for a reason. This is there in all the species you can think of. Mothers are always protective, whether it is a dog, polar bear, cat or giraffe. This mother's instinct and parental love is imbibed in all animals as well as humans so that their children are not eaten up or harmed by bigger species, and the species survives and doesn't become extinct. However, in the race towards material life, greed overtook our needs. Although not everyone is self-centred, such behaviour is becoming predominant in modern times. This is the greatest anomaly of nature! One has to grant full credit to Chanakya for having understood this more than 2,500 years ago, when interdependence prevailed, thanks to joint families.

Parents must also ensure that one sibling should never be allowed to control the finances of the family as this will antagonize others immensely at some point or the other.

3. **Enjoy Now**

Na changaat tyajeyt.

Whatever you have, enjoy it now; do not wait for much more to come in the future before you start enjoying. Chanakya pointed out that circumstances are beyond one's control or force, therefore, even though one must work hard to earn and acquire more, they should not throw away the good today for a great tomorrow—there can always be a slip between the cup and the lip.

Like most of his teachings, Chanakya gave a very practical approach to live a happy and successful life, explaining what winning actually means.

Personal Wisdom and Grooming

To enhance your own potential, it is of utmost importance that one acquires wisdom and pays attention to self-grooming as well. Chanakya, through his sutras, had a lot to say regarding these aspects.

1. **Noble Care Only for Honour**

   Addamaa dhanamichanti dhanam cha maddhyamah.
   Uttamaa maanaichanti maano hi mahaataam dhanaam.

   Here Chanakya analysed the character of people and advised us what to strive for in life. According to Chanakya, mean people only aspire to get more and more wealth; they don't care for anything else and don't even bother about how they get it. Mediocre people yearn for wealth but also care a bit about their honour and respect. However, the noble ones only aspire to gain stature in society and worry only for honour.

   Money and property are easy to get but being respected and building a reputation matters the most, which is also a tough call. There are companies who have huge assets and are very profitable, yet they do not enjoy market confidence because people do not trust them. Then, there are brands that may not have a very strong balance sheet, but they have strong brand equity only because of their reputation. Therefore, build yourself as a credible brand, as an individual and the rest will fall in place.

2. **A Noble Person Can Spread Noble Thoughts and a Wicked Person Does Not Have the Power to Sway Him/Her**

Satsagatbhavati hi saadhutaa khalaanaam, sadhnaan nahi kalsangateh khattyam, ammodham kasumbhavam bhoodev dhatte, mrindaagandhan nahi kussumaani dharyaanti.

Here Chanakya talked about satsangat, which means good company. When people sit down and discuss good things and have spiritually inclined conversations, it is called satsang—'sat' means good, 'sangat' means company. He said that the company of noble people influences the wicked positively but the wicked can never influence the noble. Hence, it is implied that noble people are stronger. In much the same way, parents give good sanskaar (values) to their children, but as time passes, some become wise and well-mannered and a few, who are not strong enough, get easily influence by bad company. In a nutshell, children must absorb the values too. Chanakya said that the soil accepts the fragrance of the flower but the flower does not accept the odour of the soil.

3. Do Not Be Naive

Naattyantam saralen bhaavyam gattvaa pashya vanasthaleem.

Chiddyante saralaastatra kubjaastishthanti paadaapah.

Never be too simple lest you want the world to take you for a ride. Innocence is often taken for dumbness and people take advantage of this simplicity. He gave the example of straight trees that get cut instead of those which grow in a haphazard manner and have thorns and bushes. Don't be too generous and kind-hearted in a world full of jackals and hounds because you will not be able to survive. Being a bit reserved, practical and, sometimes, even being curt is good as it shows that you cannot be taken for granted.

Many people who had been too kind to their business partners or relatives when it came to the division of property, have lost a lot of what actually belonged to them. I have also seen that the smart ones never part with their share in the business too generously and fight for every per cent of the share and take their pound of flesh. This is wisdom; one should not throw away everything to prove that one is a saint. Similarly, in international relations and politics, there are no permanent enemies and no permanent friends. National interest should be on top of the stack always. This is also applicable at a personal level. In business partnerships, I have witnessed that, sometimes, one partner does all the work and trusts the other for the finances and eventually he pays heavily for that.

4. **Fight the Fear**

Tavaad bhayeshuh bhetavvyaam yaadaav bhayamanaagatat.
Aagatam tu bhayam veekshaya prahartavyamshankyaa.

One can be apprehensive when danger is at a distance, but when that danger comes too close, they keep their eyes shut and expect it to disappear on its own. This is like when a pigeon shuts his eyes when he sees an approaching cat, thinking that the cat will not attack. However, in this folly, he loses his life. Chanakya said that when danger comes close, fight it with all your might. In fact, the other way of looking at it is that when you get an inkling of danger, prepare to fight and hit out with all your might when the time is right.

5. **Comfort and Perceptions are Relative**

Alirayam nalinidalamadhyama
kamalaneemakarandamadaalasah.
Vidhivishaatpradeshmupaagataah kurajpushparasam
bahu mannyate.

When you are getting drenched in rain and suddenly find a thick tree cover, you feel so happy and protected; when you are hungry, you relish a simple dish or a bowl of soup as if it is a royal treat. Similarly, when a person who has seen a life of comfort for too long (which he may not have appreciated and might have taken for granted) has to face bad days due to adverse circumstances, he realizes the importance of what he had earlier. At that time, he has to gradually accept his fallen standard of living. You may be used to an air-conditioned house, but when you come inside from the heat and there is no power to switch the AC on, you love to sit under a fan which runs on your inverter. This is the theory of relativity or relative happiness. Even Albert Einstein said, 'When you sit with a nice girl for two hours you think it's only a minute, but when you sit on a hot stove for a minute, you think it's two hours. That's relativity.' The corollary being—appreciate what you have, as these good days may change for the worse. Giving an example, Chanakya said that a bee that had once got to live amongst the tasty lotus flowers starts to relish the nectar of even the kuruj flower when it is hungry.

When India had to face partition in 1947, people who migrated from Lahore and Karachi to Delhi and others part of the country had left their flourishing businesses and had to live in India as refugees. But they learnt to live in what was available to them under those circumstances.

6. How to Enhance Whatever You Have

Guno bhooshayatey roopma sheelam bhooshyatey kulam.
Siddhirbhooshyatey viddyaam bhogo bhooshyatey dhanam.

In this sutra, Chanakya spoke about the power to augment your gifts and use them appropriately to your advantage. Don't underutilize your gifts and waste what you have.

For example, if you belong to a good family, then good manners, sophistication and grace will enhance your glory and stature. This is usually demonstrated by the royals who always do things immaculately and in style. One can make out from one's behaviour what kind of upbringing that person has had. Similarly, virtues and good attitude will enhance the beauty of a man as well as a woman. If you are educated, do your job diligently and demonstrate perfection and punctuality, and only then will your education take you further in your career. There is no point of having wealth if you do not enjoy it. Use it wisely; don't throw away your money. Strike a balance between being a miser and being a spendthrift. Yet, don't waste away the gift of wealth by being a miser; use it for your pleasure sensibly. This also implies that don't keep working on multiplying your wealth, but enjoy it too.

7. **Don't Be Jealous**

Mookhahanaam pandita dveshyaadhanaanaam mahadhaanaa.

Vaaraangana kuleelanam subhganam cha durbhage.

The poor are envious of the rich, prostitutes are envious of women married into good families, fools are unhappy with scholars and widows are envious of those whose husbands are alive.

You should aspire to have what others have but nursing envy will make your life miserable and will impede your progress.

8. **If You Are Weak, You Must Enter into a Pact with a Stronger Opponent**

Hiyaamaan saandhee kurveet.

Never take the stronger adversary or competitor on face value. Evaluate your strength, and if you are no match, it is better not to fight; instead, go for a treaty which works for both. Many people make it an ego issue and take on more than they can handle. This is a sure-shot recipe for defeat and self-destruction. In life, one must understand how much is too much. A winning strategy is not based on hunches or rhetoric; it is based on data, calculation and assessment of your own strengths as well as those of the adversary. If you feel there is something which is beyond your capability, then you may as well compromise and not attempt to handle it. Students who are weak in calculations and accounts should not attempt to go for chartered accountancy exams as they will get frustrated.

9. **Company Matters**

Gunwada shrayanigurnopee gunee bhavataa.

If you stay with learned people and keep wise company, you will automatically pick up good things. Organization culture is about selecting the right people who can boost each other's strength. My experience as a teacher tells me that in a batch of hundred students, if eighty are good, then they can pull up the weak twenty during the course. But, if you reverse it, then the twenty good ones will also fall prey to bad company. As the head of a management school, I would always say that if the eighty good students decide to take along the rest, the batch will perform very well, and that was always the result.

10. **Don't Oblige a Mean and Wicked Person**

Upkaro gyanoyehshkartavya.

Mean people are always ungrateful and, therefore, one should never oblige such people, as they do not even understand what an obligation is. This is one of the important lessons of life because if you need to do a favour, do it to someone who would feel obliged and would be able to return the favour whenever you need his help. Life is give and take, and that is how relations also work. Therefore, never become emotional and do a favour to a person who is 'ehsan faramosh' or ungrateful. The flip side to this is that you must always remember a favour done to you. Try to return that favour whenever you get a chance and always acknowledge the person who did a favour to you.

This way you will be able to ask for a favour from him some other time in the future as well. This also builds your credibility in the circle in which you move. Others also view you as a good person who remembers and acknowledges a favour.

Money Matters

Many preach that money is not important and it is not everything. Yes, money is not everything, but adequate money is required to live a decent, comfortable life. One must therefore be careful in saving as well as spending money. One must have a dependable means of earning as well.

1. **Save for a Rainy Day**

   Aapadartham dhanam rakshechayashcha kimaapadah.
   Kadaachichachalitas laxmi sanditaapi vinashyati.

   It is good to spend on yourself, but one should save enough for times of need. Riches can be destroyed in a jiffy, therefore, keep a portion of your earnings as an investment. In today's context, make a home for yourself, buy some assets such as shares and bonds, and keep some cash in the bank which should neither be touched nor invested unwisely.

   I see a lot of young people, who are getting high salaries, throw caution out of the window as if they would never lose their job or the industry will keep paying them the same way, giving them bonuses and increments every year. This is never going to be true. Even if you are good, at some point, the industry may not do well. Industry and economy also move in a cyclic fashion with ups and downs. You should be prepared for the downside of the cycle; in today's age, this is more relevant, as there is nothing like a secure job. For example, in the IT industry, more people are hired than required. Then, till they actually get projects to execute, they put a substantial number of people on the 'bench' where one is paid for doing nothing. This is like having a football team of fifteen players where only eleven play at a time and when there is a foul or an injury, only then do the other players get a chance to play.

Similarly, in the industry, since you are paid regularly, you feel like you are having a ball. You spend all that you earn and buy expensive cars and homes with easy loans on hefty EMIs. But, when there is a shake-up in the industry, you lose your job. Now, you don't know what to do and how to pay all those loans.

That is not fair at all. One should follow the old saying— cut your coat according to the cloth that you have.

Therefore, manage your finances well and keep a good amount for the tough times, if an when they come.

2. **Don't Waste Your Charitable Portion**
    Vritha vrishteeh samudreshu vrithaa tripteshu bhojanaam.
    Vritha daanam dhanadhyeshu vritha deepo divapee cha.
    We give gifts to those who don't need gifts. In fact, people who have enough get tired of getting gifts. For example, on festivals like Diwali or Christmas, people give boxes of

sweets and cakes to friends and relatives, and in the end, most people have their refrigerators full of these items which some even throw away. During weddings, people waste money in giving gifts which are not even required by the couple. Chanakya said that heavy rainfall is useless over the sea; similarly, giving alms to the rich and burning a lamp during the day also make no sense.

Therefore, one should give gifts to those who need them and would be able to use them. Instead of giving an expensive coat to a rich man, one may as well give ten blankets to the poor who need them in winters. Of late, there is a sensible trend during weddings of people writing on the invitation card—'No gifts please'. It saves everyone the trouble. I also feel that people shouldn't waste money on pomp and show for every function or celebration. Instead, they should use that money for a better cause or even save that for some other purpose.

3. **Spend If You Have the Money**

Kimatyaa kriyaatey laxammyaa yaa vadhooriv kevallaa.
Yaa tu veshyew saamaanmyapathikairapi bhujhyatey.

If you earn, you must enjoy that money. There is no point keeping the money locked in the bank or in a vault. There are people who waste their money and burn up their resources and, in the end, land up as paupers; on the other hand, there are some misers who do not even live in comfort when they have the resources.

There is a difference between being frugal and being stingy and a miser. There are rich celebrities who won't let go of their money. For example, Michael Jordan has retired, but he's still very rich. In fact, he's the highest-paid athlete in history. He earned more than $1.7 billion during his playing days. But he's not a big spender. He's actually notorious for being cheap and a bad tipper. According to former rival Charles Barkley, Jordan also refused to give money to the homeless.

Lady Gaga is a celebrity who has made a significant amount of money over the past several years—money that she doesn't part with easily. She loves coupons; it seems like a strange habit for a multimillionaire, but she even likes to bargain when shopping for clothes!

Sarah Jessica Parker whose net worth is more than $90 million is very frugal and also doesn't mind recycling or buying second-hand clothes for her family.

'He is richest who is content with the least, for content is the wealth of nature.'

—*Socrates*

In a Nutshell: The Importance of Dealing with Yourself

1. **Self-assessment**: This is the first step towards self-improvement. Understanding your own strengths and weaknesses is very important.
2. **Need for Friends**: One needs a support system and, therefore, needs friends and family.
3. **Add Value to Your Job**: Your personal conduct must be impeccable. You must add value to your job and also to what you own or inherit.
4. **Matters of the Ego**: It is also important to keep your ego in check and not to blow your own trumpet. Let others praise you.
5. **Deal with Your Enemy**: Handle your enemy tactfully. If he is weak, you can fight him but if he is strong, deal with him diplomatically.

6. **Don't Break Rules That You Make**: Remain dedicated to your work and aims that you wish to fulfil.

7. **Time and Timing Are Important**: Everything should begin at an appropriate time. Never change your time plan, which has been chalked out beforehand.

8. **Never Panic Because of Natural Calamities**: If you face a natural calamity, remain strong. Those who take this as a part of life and move on, definitely succeed.

9. **Handle Your Boss**: Dress up as per the occasion and be of some use to the person you report to.

10. **Never Be Ungrateful to Those Who Were Good to You**: Always be grateful to people who helped you during your difficult days.

11. **The Human Mind Works in Two Spheres**: One is associated with emotions and the other is the rational part of our thinking. One has to intelligently shift between these two, according to the situation, to move on in life smoothly.

12. **Handle People with Care**: Love is a powerful tool which can mellow down people you are dealing with. Never be too harsh with people.

13. **Understand the Basic Psyche of People Whom You Deal with**: People who have bad intentions always doubt others' intentions. Those who are cheats and dishonest always see others as the same.

14. **Beware of Ungrateful People:** Don't oblige a mean and a wicked person, as such people don't even understand what obligation is.

15. **Money is an Important Part of One's Life As Long As It Has Been Earned Honestly:** Use money with utmost care. There are big film stars who didn't invest their money properly, lost everything and died as paupers.

5

POWER OF CHARACTER

'Nearly all men can stand adversity, but if you want to test a man's character, give him power.'

–Abraham Lincoln

One cannot undermine the power of character as a contributor to one's success. You can be intelligent, hard-working and have a sharp intellect, but if you do not have the strength of character and moral qualities, you will not be able to go very far. Character defines your nature, mentality and disposition. Chanakya gave a lot of importance to this aspect of a person and recommended a strong moral fibre not only for kings and leaders but also for every individual vying for success.

He explained what all one needs to to build a good and strong character. Great men in every field have had a strong character. The one thing common to Abraham Lincoln, Winston Churchill, Mahatma Gandhi and Nelson Mandela is the strength of their characters.

Here are some of the ways Chanakya suggested to build character:

1. **Virtue Enhances Stature and Not High Position**

   Gunairuttamattaam yaanti nochairaasansansthitai.
   Praasaadshikharasthoapi kim kaako garudaayate.

   Chanakya beautifully presented this important point related to virtuous people. He unequivocally stated that even if you make a crow sit on the high pedestal of the royal palace, he cannot become as mighty as the Garuda, the lord of the birds as per Hindu mythology. Therefore, one must add value to the chair he occupies by his great qualities and not just be proud of a position he has been given. This also hints at dynastic rules where just because of your bloodline, you may get a position of power which you actually do not deserve. There are hundreds of examples from the entertainment industry as well as politics where people get everything easily on the plate because of their parents but are not able to prove themselves later.

2. **Donation and Helping Others Is an Indicator of Good Character**

   Aarteshu vipreshu dayaannivihschechaddhena yaha svalpamupaiti dannam.

   Anantparam samupaiti daanam yaddeeyate tanna labhed dvijebhyah.

   People of character and good upbringing help these who are in need. Chanakya said that if you have money and might, you must help people in distress and it will come back to you many times over. People don't do charity to get returns, but this is the law of nature. Across the world, especially in the modern era, one sees foundations created by industrialists and educators to help the destitute. The Ford Foundation, the Bill Gates and Melinda Gates Foundation, the Bharati Foundation for Education are all examples of institutions created for public good. Many celebrities go out of their way to set up charitable trusts and get involved with organizations to help others. Many start their own NGOs to do this in an organized way.

   Chanakya also said that if you help the worthy, then it is all the more better, as they will become successful one day and carry your torch forward by helping others. Thus, the legacy of such charity survives forever. He also advised that one should donate liberally and as much as one can afford to.

3. **Respecting Women**

    Raajpatnee guroh patnee mitrapatnee tathaivcha.
    Patneemaataa svamaataa cha panchaittah mattarah
    smritah.

    Many people, including kings, ministers, the rich and the mighty as well as common men have disrespected women. In recent days, many celebrities, industrialists as well as people in high positions have been accused of sexual exploitation and abuse. Many have fallen from their high pedestal and landed on the ground with a thud because of their one such mistake. Chanakya had remarked that every woman deserves respect. Treating them any other way is sinful. Men of character stay away from such behaviour. One blotch on your credentials is enough for people to keep you at arm's length for the rest of your life and it is difficult to find a way out.

    As Giuseppe Mazzini had said, 'Love and respect a woman. Look to her not only for comfort, but for strength and inspiration and the doubling of your intellectual and moral powers. Blot out from your mind any idea of superiority; you have none.'

4. **Men of Character Demonstrate Nobility Even During Their Bad Days**

   Chhinoapi chandantarun jaahati gandham.

   Vridhoapi vaaranpatrin jaahati leelanaam.

   Yantrarpito madurtaam na jaahati.

   The greatest people show grace under pressure and during testing times. A leader is supposed to take along her/his people in good as well as bad times. Chanakya said that even if a sandalwood tree is cut off, it still gives off fragrance. Men of character do have a charisma which doesn't fade even in defeat; they can always bounce back. Giving another practical example, Chanakya said that sugarcane, even if crushed, gives us its sweet juice.

   Therefore, people who maintain their noble ways even during bad times are considered great as their conduct during adversities is the litmus test of their character.

5. **Beauty and Strength Lie in Charity**

   Dannen paanirn tu kankanen snaanen shuddhirna tu chandanen.

   Maanen triptrin tu bhojanen gyaanen muktirna tu mandanen.

   People of character do not feel elated when they are being fed by their well-wishers; they feel happy when they are being honoured by them. Honour is more important than sumptuous food and gifts. In fact, an Olympic gold medal may not cost much, but look at the laurels it brings to the player. Similarly, awards like Padma Vibhushan and Padma Bhushan are more to do with stature than materialistic rewards. That is true for any recognition. Chanakya also went one step ahead by saying that the state of nirvana or moksha is attained by knowledge and not by self-decoration or by collection material for yourself. Moksha is being desire-less, whereas collecting materialistic stuff is actually the outcome of greed.

People who remain free of yearning are definitely worthy of praise for their strong character.

In recent times, one can observe the behaviour of the rich and the mighty in this context. There are rich people who treat their employees, drivers or servants with dignity. But there are others who get so drunk with power and money that they misbehave with people who do not matter to them. This also happens in our country where politicians and their children think they own the law and misbehave even with public servants. This is never appreciated and people scoff at such behaviour. Judge a person by how he behaves with those who do not matter to him.

6. **Purity and Goodness Shine More If Possessed by a Wise Person**

Vivekinmunuprapato guno yaati manogyataam.
Sutaraam rattnamaabhaati chaameekarniyojitam.

Rectitude and morality add value to a wise man just like an expensive gem adds to the beauty of gold base that it is embedded in.

As the Hindi saying goes, *'Soney pe suhaaga'*, it is like the icing on the cake. If you are wise and knowledgeable and also have virtues like morality, humility and honesty, it is a strong combination of character and knowledge. Look at Abraham Lincoln or Mahatma Gandhi. Both had knowledge acquired through education and self-learning. They rose to the heights of glory because they also had strong characters in terms of honesty and integrity.

7. **Do Not Be Selfish While Dealing with People or with the Environment**

Yatrodakastratra vassantee haanssaa sthataiv shushkaam parrittyajanti na haanssatullyen naren bhavyaam punaastaayaajaanathy punassraashraantaah.

Chanakya always gave simple examples to illustrate his point. He dwelled on good character by giving the example of swans that live in a pond full of water, but if the water dries up, they desert it.

He was implying that a person of character does not leave his friends and alliances based on which side the wind is blowing; he sticks to his alliances and groups of well-wishers through thick and thin. He advised that people should not be like the opportunistic swans who would possibly return to the same pond once it gets filled with rainwater.

However, in politics, there are no permanent friends or enemies, as the saying goes. Politicians look at their personal gains and advantage in a situation, even dumping their parties whom they were loyal to for decades.

This is a strong parameter which has to be viewed as an integrity issue in the job market in today's age, though human nature has been corruptible and selfish from the beginning. You should not leave a company which has trained you and maintained you over the years just because someone has offered you a better pay package. This is an unfortunate trend which I am sure the human resources department of companies keep a watch on.

8. **If You Are the Custodian of Someone's Property or Wealth, Be Honest**

Apardhaanani nikshaiptu kewalam swartham.

This is one of the most important points in terms of the

integrity and character of a person. If someone trusts you and makes you the custodian of his property, then do ensure that you guard it as you would guard your own wealth. This is the trust factor, which is one of the most important parameters within the construct of character. Many times, the power of attorney for a property has been misused by someone the owner trusted. Not only friends, but even siblings have done this to each other. The additional point here would be to ensure you don't completely trust people with financial matters.

Another case in point is the banking system. For instance, a bank is the custodian of public money. They are supposed to guard it and ensure they don't end up losing it through any malpractices. This has been a recent trend where non-performing assets of banks shot through the roof because of a bad loan policy. Even in a personal capacity, lending can be a problem when one is not sure of the potential borrower's character.

In today's scenario, things don't look very good because most people have lost their moral fibre. There are more crooks than honest people. During the times of Chanakya, things may have been better because most people had character and were bothered about their reputation. Today, we have instances of industrialists who took loans from banks amounting to thousands of crores and very smartly moved out of the country to dodge the system. They have the cheek to defy the system and show two fingers to the government too. Never ever do business or any financial transactions with people of dubious character.

9. **Avoid Backbiting and Talking Ill of Someone in His Absence**

Pishnoo shrotta putradaarerprati tyaajyaatey.

Backbiting is playing dirty politics. In case you want to talk of someone, then talk about him to others in his presence, and in a dignified manner. Backbiting becomes like a Chinese whispers game and the same thing might one day come back to you, stinging harder than you could even imagine. People who backbite are never liked and always end up in trouble at some point or the other. To be a team player and gain respect in an organization or among friends, never indulge in backbiting—these are the golden words you must remember.

Chanakya even mentioned that those who backbite are deserted by their own family. It is not very uncommon to see relatives and friends talk ill of their own kin in their absence. When they get caught, it creates embarrassment and ill will. So much so that at times, families break apart.

The rule of the thumb is to be frank and speak to the person concerned directly rather than talking behind his back.

10. **Never Rely on Lawbreakers**
Maryaadaateet na kadaacheedapi wishwaseit.
Never trust a person who breaks the law or cheats others as he cannot be relied upon. If he can cheat others, he can cheat you as well.

One can observe this at an organizational level too. Good companies like Tata have a code of conduct for their employees across the board. Such companies never ask their employees to do illegal things and ask them to go as per the law and ethical code. Such organizations pay their dues well, pay taxes as desired and give value for money to the customers. It works both ways—the company never cheats you and would never ask you to cheat either. Many times, employees leave a dubious company because they are asked to do wrong things on behalf of the company which they are not comfortable with.

This exodus happens at all levels—from a purchase manager to the CEO. People who do not toe the line of such organizations are actually men of great character.

11. **Never Betray Others**

Awishwasteshoo vishwaso na kartavya.

You should never rely on a person who is a known betrayer. He may give hundreds of reasons to justify what he did in the past, but it is not at all safe to trust him. Jaichand, a famous king of Ayodhya and Varanasi, had major political and family differences with Prithviraj Chauhan, ruler of the Sapadalakha territory (in present-day northwestern India). Mughal king Mohammad Ghori wanted to capture Indian territory and invaded Prithviraj's kingdom. This happened because Jaichand had given away the secrets of Prithviraj Chauhan's battle plans to Ghori and ensured that the Hindu king was defeated by a Muslim invading enemy. He had promised to join Prithviraj to fight Ghori together, but at the last minute, ditched him there too. In the end, he lost all that he had.

Keep people like Jaichand at arm's length and never trust them because they can backstab you anytime.

Never betray a friend or people you work for. Communication today is so fast that if you have been labelled a backstabber, word will spread so quickly that you may never ever get a job again or even be able to start your own work.

'If you have integrity, nothing else matters. If you don't have integrity, nothing else matters.'

—*Alan Kooi Simpson*

In a Nutshell: The Power of Character

1. **Success**: One cannot undermine the power of character as a contributor to one's success. You can be intelligent, hard-working as well as have a sharp intellect, but if you do not have the strength of character and moral qualities, you will not be able to go very far.

2. **Leadership**: Great men in every field have had a strong personal character. Abraham Lincoln, Winston Churchill, Mahatma Gandhi and Nelson Mandela—all demonstrated a great and often unique character which, in many cases, became their trademark.

3. **Charity**: Men and women of great character help others through charity and good deeds. Good men respect women and noble people show stability during bad times.

4. **Wisdom**: Morality and righteousness add value to a wise man. If you are wise and knowledgeable and also have virtues like morality, humility and honesty, you have a

strong combination of character and knowledge.

5. **Wealth and Honesty**: Be honest to the last rupee, never backbite and never be selfish.

6. **Loyalty**: Never rely on a person of weak character. Also, never betray others or rely on a known betrayer.

7. **Value Addition**: Add value to the position you acquire. While sitting on a throne, a king must not rely on the price of the throne but must add value to it by his virtues, deeds and good character.

6

WISDOM AND COMMON SENSE

'Common sense is genius dressed in its working clothes.'

—Ralph Waldo Emerson

I have always been intrigued by the expression 'common sense'; therefore, I wanted to delve deeper into the ocean of human sensibilities and conventional intelligence as we perceive it, and try to make some sense of common sense! I also felt that there is a direct link between common sense and wisdom. Let me first establish this fact that they are two sides of the same coin.

Now sample this idea about common sense by Jim Taylor, adjunct professor at the University of San Francisco—'Common sense, defined as the "sound judgement derived from experience rather than study", is one of the most revered qualities in America. It evokes images of early and simpler times in which industrious men and women built our country into what it is today. People with common sense are seen as reasonable, down to earth, reliable, and practical.'

I would pick on two words from the above statement—reliable and practical. The above statement is not only true for the US but is a globally accepted truth that applies to all of us, irrespective of what profession we pursue. It is also a fact that common sense is not very common because had that been the case, people wouldn't have made the same mistakes as often as they do or the kind of decisions they make almost every day. People wouldn't buy things they can't afford. They wouldn't smoke or eat junk food. They wouldn't gamble. Students wouldn't bunk classes, subordinates wouldn't abuse and fight with their bosses, husbands and wives wouldn't have showdowns.

All these are so simple to understand and are common knowledge, like people who don't fight with their bosses are practical and reliable as subordinates.

Let us say you employ four people. Out of them, whom will you give a critical task to handle? I am sure you will pick someone who you have faith in and who is dependable. This means that person exudes confidence and you can rely on him. Having done that you would also like to assess who is more practical in approaching a tricky situation or handling something that he encounters out of the blue. He is smart enough to take the best option out of the available ones. Instead of complicating matters, he can simplify the problem and solve it in a better way.

I would call this 'raw intelligence' and this may even be possessed by those who may not be well-read or qualified or not even experienced in a particular field.

I feel common sense relates to innocence and simplicity as well.

If you ask a class 5 student to tell you which title would he prefer, out of the options you give him, for a book, there is a huge probability for him to give an answer which would be spot on. He uses his gut feeling; thus, one could say that common sense also resembles or is a close cousin of gut feeling. Gut feeling, as per definition, is 'an instinct or intuition; an immediate or basic feeling or reaction without a logical rationale'. Most of the philosophical statements by thinkers like Socrates, Plato or Aristotle have been accepted over centuries across the world because they are so simple and appealing to all. It is also important to note that we call these thinkers wise people. Therefore, wisdom and common sense both converge at a point—they are simple, practical and take a straightforward approach. It would be fair to say that wisdom resembles common sense or, to some extent, both are as good as each other.

Thomas Edison used to have a unique way of selecting engineers for his corporation. He would ask questions which had very simple answers. Almost all the candidates would opt for a rigorous engineering route, but there would always be one odd fellow who would do it in the simplest manner and Edison would eventually select him.

For instance, he asked this question to dozens of engineers who had applied for a job, 'Here is a shell of a bulb, please calculate its volume.' One bulb shell was handed over to each one of them. Almost everyone went for a vernier calliper to take the dimensions of the bulb and used complex equations to come up with the volume of the bulb which was theoretically very close to the actual volume. One guy walked up to a mug of water placed on the nearby table, filled up the shell of the bulb with the water, picked up a measuring beaker, poured the water out of the bulb into the beaker, read the scale on the beaker and gave out the exact volume of the bulb. This guy was selected. Now, this had nothing to do with his engineering qualification and training. This was common sense or raw intelligence and that is what is most cherished in creativity, production and problem-solving.

'The three great essentials to achieve anything worthwhile are: hard work, stick-to-itiveness and common sense.'

—*Thomas Edison*

There is another example of common sense from the literary world. Nigel Newton, the founder and chief executive of Bloomsbury Publishing, revealed in an interview that the first *Harry Potter* manuscript was rejected by all of his major rivals. It was only because of the pester-power of his daughter Alice, who had read a chapter and demanded more, that finally convinced the publisher that he had a winner on his hands!

The London-based publisher was almost the last chance for J.K. Rowling to see *Harry Potter and the Philosopher's Stone* in print, having been rejected by several publishers, some of them big ones. Newton was given the manuscript by the publishing agent of J.K. Rowling. He took it home, but, instead of settling down with it himself, he handed it to his daughter Alice, then eight years old.

'She came down from her room an hour later, glowing,' Newton recalls, 'saying, "Dad, this is so much better than anything else." She nagged and nagged me in the following months, wanting to see what came next.' Newton made out a cheque to Rowling for just £2,500, which has since proved one of the wisest investments in publishing history.

What do you call this? Common sense of a child and the wisdom of her father.

The dictionary meaning of wisdom goes as follows—'the ability to use your knowledge and experience to make good decisions and judgements.'

The end result of wisdom and common sense is the same— good judgement. Hence, QED, or 'quod erat demonstrandum,' which means, 'what was to be shown'.

Putting it mathematically—if A equals B and B equals C, then A equals C. Simple?

Chanakya demonstrated this through his teachings all the time. His wisdom, encapsulated in his sutras, is a treat for every mind which can grasp a grass-roots-level idea; one doesn't require a high IQ or great academic prowess to understand these.

Now, let me explain something which is possibly being observed by every reader of this book—'understanding a verse or sutra is common sense and applying the teachings of the sutra in real life is wisdom'. As mentioned before, 'Reading and understanding a story is knowledge, and understanding the moral of the story is wisdom.' If you observe both the statements, you will realize they closely resemble each other in essence.

'Life is a boomerang. What you give, you get.'

—*Dale Carnegie*

Now, let us see some sutras from *Chanakya Neeti* which talk about common sense and wisdom.

Karma and Actions

1. **Man Takes Actions and Has to Bear the Consequences**
   Svayam karma karottyaattamaa svayam tattphalamashnute.
   Svayam bhramati sansaare svayam tasmaaddvimuchchayate.
   'As you sow so shall you reap,' says the Bible. Looking at it in more detail, your actions determine your future; whatever happens is because of what you did in the past and you will have to face the consequences yourself in the future; that means you, in a nutshell, are responsible for your actions. Karma is a Sanskrit word meaning 'action'. However, it embraces the whole meaning of living. The law of karma occupies a central position in Indian philosophy as well. According to Indian philosophy, we

are because of our karma. Thus, our karma or actions or deeds (both good and bad) decide our future in this as well as in the next life. There is a balance sheet maintained by nature or the almighty, and it takes into account your good and bad deeds. Another way of looking at it is that at any given point in your life, you are what you have learnt cumulatively till then. Therefore, you act according to your beliefs learned from your environment, family, etc. This implies that you are doing what you have learnt and hence things cannot be changed by you. Karma is not a fixed entity, which means you can change the course of your life by consciously taking actions using your own logic and intelligence—that is how man is different than other living beings; he can decipher between what is right and what is wrong.

This is exactly what Chanakya said—you are responsible for your actions, therefore, act after due diligence, and intelligently.

If you murder someone, then you are responsible for it and you will be sent to jail. Similarly, when you do a good thing, you will be rewarded for it.

This is so simple to understand—is this not common sense? And, this is also wisdom passed on to us by every noble person and religion.

2. **No Matter Where You Are, the Consequences of Your Actions Will Always Catch Up with You**

Yathaa dhenu sahastreshu vattso gachhati maatram.

Tathaa yachcha kritam karma kartaaramanugachchati.

This is an extension of the theory of karma and simply means that whether you do good or bad, you will always have to face its consequences, be it a reward or a punishment. Chanakya said that as a calf is able to find his mother amongst thousands of cows, the consequences of your actions will find you too; there is no escape.

But, sometimes, in our greed, ambition, anger or simply when emotions get the better of us, we throw logic out of the window and our stupid acts result in a backlash or punishment.

Therefore, it is wise to act only after due diligence and after ensuring that our actions do not land us in trouble.

Values and Moksha: Your Road to Happiness

If you want to live happily, you must live by moral values and must keep your greed in check. You must have aspirations, but they must not overpower you. You must have value-based principles and stick to the truth, as truth always wins. A lie may give you temporary gratification, but one day you will get caught. You may bluff now, but it would not be possible to get away all the time. Count your blessings and look at people who don't even have what you have. You may be driving an air-conditioned car, but a man of your age may be riding a cycle next to you in the heat and dust. Think for a minute what he is going through while you are travelling in comfort. When you witness death and suffering, you begin to understand that it is not worth running after money and material comforts more than you require.

1. Truth Is the Most Important Entity

Sattyen dhaaryate prithvee sttyen tapate ravi, sattyen vaati vaayushcha sarvam sattye prathishthitam.

Chanakya laid emphasis on truth to such an extent that he said that it is truth that stabilizes everything in the world, and is all-pervasive. It alone establishes order in creation. There is no doubt that truth always wins, and one, therefore, should follow the correct and honest path in life.

Again, in modern life, we resort to being tricksters, dishonest and untruthful, and that is the reason for our rotting society. In the ancient times, people had strong morals and seldom told a lie or duped anyone; that is why it was called Satyug. Today, we are living in Kalyug, where we are bombarded with fake news and deceit all the time. It is difficult to discern right from wrong. Look at what is happening on social media and mainstream conventional media—it is becoming increasingly difficult to trust anyone.

Life would be so much better if we could trust people, politicians and government officials as well as businessmen. How do you feel when you are cheated, or someone sells you a product or a service based on a lie? You will not like something of inferior quality when you have paid a good amount for it. For example, when you book a hotel by seeing the pictures that are displayed on the hotel's website, you expect the rooms to be as shown. But if you find the rooms to be substandard and different from what you paid for, you will complain to the hotel staff and even seek a refund. You will also not recommend that hotel to any of your friends.

A hotel can dupe you once, but not every time, as people will post negative feedback about it.

2. Shun All Sensual Attractions

Muktimisachasi cheetal vishayan tyajee.
Kshmaarjvadyaashauchcham sattyaam piyooshvat pibb.
This appears a bit preachy, but it is a fact of life. If you

want to be happy and liberated, detach yourself from worldly, materialistic things. It may not be possible for us to give up all good things in life, but if we do not give too much importance to these things, then our life will be a lot better. If you give too much importance to something, then it starts troubling you. For instance, if you want a particular job and you don't get it, in spite of your best attempts, what would you do? You would either sulk about it or you would try to take the rejection in your stride and move on. This constant fixation on something is like poison in your system and the earlier you take it out, the better it is. Chanakya, through the above sutra, suggested that we should cultivate the spirit of forgiveness, compassion and contentment. The idea of '*dil maange more*' (the heart demands more) is exactly opposite to this ethos. As someone said, '*Har ghar mein ek kamra kam hai*' (according to the owner, there is one room less than required in every house). If you have a two-bedroom house, you want an extra study room. Once you get it, you want another bedroom, then five bedrooms and then a garage, a gym; then, you want a two-storey bungalow, and this list goes on and on. Therefore, try to simplify your life and you will live happily ever after.

3. **We Are Enlightened When We See Suffering and Death**

Dharmakkhyaane shmashaane cha roginaam yaa matirbhavet.

Saa sarvadaiv thishttbechet ko na muchyate bandhannat.

Chanakya said that one understands that the material world has little to offer. When one sees people who are sick or when one goes for cremation to the burial ground, one realizes that all that one has been running for has little meaning.

Helen Keller said, 'I cried because I had no shoes until I met a man who had no feet.'

If you have ever been to a cremation ground, you may have read words of wisdom written all over the walls: 'You will leave everything behind and not be able to take anything with you in your final journey' or 'you will be remembered by your friends and relatives only by your good deeds'. In that environment, it then dawns on you that ultimately you will also be gone one day. I remember someone saying at the cremation ground, '*Sau saal ka saaman ikatthaa kara, lekin kal ka pataa nahin*' (You accumulate stuff for the next hundred years, but you are not even sure of tomorrow).

'Family is not an important thing, it's everything.'

—*Michael J. Fox*

Family and Children

A happy family brings prosperity, satisfaction and happiness in life. Chanakya lays emphasis on raising children appropriately and with care. He says that one would be lucky to have good children. He also says that all children cannot be equally good, but you must not discriminate.

1. **Bring up Your Children with Prudence**

   Laalyet panchavarshani dashavarshaani taadyet.
   Praapte tu shodashe varshe putram mitravadaacharet.

   Chanakya gave sound and practical advice regarding how to bring up children, especially your son. Many of us go wrong in this aspect and regret it later. He said that till your son is five years old, treat him like a child and shower all your affections on him. Thereafter, for the next ten years, be strict with him, discipline him and reprimand and censure him according to the requirement. When he turns sixteen, treat him as your friend and give him some freedom to make his own choices. When a boy turns sixteen, he is able to take his own decisions, and parents should encourage their children to always discuss important things with them at this age. There should be a sense of participation and responsibility. When you give someone responsibility, you will see that he automatically delivers the results.

2. **An Incompetent Son Is a Liability**

Eken shuskvrikshen dahiyamaanen vahinnanna.
Dahyate taddvanam sarva kuputren kulam yathaa.

One bad son can ruin the entire family and jeopardize its happiness. Chanakya compared this to a jungle fire that starts with just one dry tree catching fire, which spreads through the entire jungle, burning everything to ashes.

One doesn't have to go too far—examine your own family or some close friends, and you will realize that often there is one black sheep in the family who makes life hell for others.

This also gets linked to the previous point that it is important to give your children a good, healthy childhood, educate them and make them responsible human beings. As parents, you must do your bit to bring up the children properly and leave the rest to god. But, once you do your bit, nature and god support you automatically. A happy and prosperous family is essential for your ultimate success. There is no point in earning millions when you have children who will make you unhappy and destroy your peace of mind.

3. It Is Better to Lose a Foolish Son

Moorkhashchiraayurjaatoapi tassmaattjaataannmrito varam.
Mritahsa chalpadukhaaya vavajjeevam jado dahet.

Although a bit too harsh, Chanakya stated nothing but the bitter truth. He said it is better for a foolish son to die early, because death gives grief only once, but if he lives, his foolish actions will cause pain and agony throughout his parents' life. One may have heard several parents, who have been troubled by their sons because of their foolish and unscrupulous actions, cursing, 'Why did I ever give birth to you! I wish I had no son. I would have been better without a child.'

4. Educate Your Children

Maataa shatruh pitaa vairee yen baalo na pathitaha.
Na shobhate sabhaa maddhye hansamddhye bako yathaa.

Chanakya stated that an uneducated child is like a crow amongst swans and he will stand out in society like a sore thumb. It is the duty of the parents to give their children the best education possible. Parents who do not make efforts to educate their children are like their enemy. This is a very important aspect of development, and that is why parents who are well-wishers of their children pay close attention to them to ensure that they get a good education. It is worth spending on their education than on anything else.

Fortunately, today, even the poorest of the poor understand the importance of education and also that prosperity can only be achieved through good education. It is unfortunate for those parents who spend their hard-earned money on children's education, yet, they do not make appropriate use of these opportunities. Such children repent and, at a later stage in life, they also become troublesome for their old parents.

5. **Prosperity Comes to a Happy Family**

Moorkha yaatra na poojyante dhanayam yatra susanchitam.
Dampattyoh kalaho naasti tatra shree suayamaagata.

A home has happiness, peace and prosperity only if the husband and wife have mutual respect for each other and have no fights and differences amongst them. A home should have food and eatables in abundance for it to remain prosperous. Even our grandparents always said that one should stock enough food at home so that even if ten guests arrive, they could be fed. This, according to them, brings 'barkat' to a home, which means 'prosperity and abundance'. A home will also remain happy if the family doesn't entertain fools and men of low integrity and honour.

Unfortunately, today we have little time to be at home, and due to self-created stress, most couples quarrel. There are homes where you have every materialistic comfort, yet people are not happy, as the atmosphere is always tense and people snap at each other at the drop of a hat. Divorces are likely when there is little or no understanding between the husband and wife, or when they are self-centred. Therefore, along with having materialistic comforts, mental peace is also essential. Partners should avoid inviting negativity by associating with people who lack the strength of character; one should never let them come into one's personal space, that is, one's home.

6. **Siblings May Have Different Characteristics**
   Ekodarsamuddhootaa ek nakshatru jaatakaa.
   Na bhavanti samaasheele yathaa badrikantakaah.
   Have you ever noticed that siblings—even though they

live under the same roof, eat the same food and study in the same school—may differ drastically in nature, and choose widely divergent professions? They have the same upbringing, yet they are so different! Chanakya said that parents should not expect all their children to be identical, be it in their performance or their achievements. He also said that parents should not differentiate or draw comparisons, as it will create problems amongst siblings. He said that a palm tree has fruits and thorns on the same branch, and the tree accepts and supports both of them. To keep a family together, it is important to take the bright and not-so-bright together and accept them as they are.

7. **Lazy People Can't Handle or Multiply Their Inheritance**
   Na Aalasya Rakshit Vivardhatey.

   There is an old saying in Hindi—'*Agar sapoot hoga to apne aap kamayega, aur agar kapoot hoga to sab barbad kar dega* (If your child is good and hard-working, he will make an empire for himself, but if he is lazy and good-for-nothing, he will destroy whatever you give him or bequeath to him after your death).

   As the head of a management institute, I observed that the parents of several students would tell them that the idea of an MBA was to make them job-worthy, that they would never have to ask or beg for a job, and that jobs would come to them! Second, in case you have your own business and your ward wants to join you, he should be able to double your business in the next three years. This also gets linked to the earlier sutra where Chanakya talked about good education for children and its importance in the overall well-being of the family.

8. Grief and Disease Are a Part of Life

Kassya doshah kule naasti vyaadhinaa ko na peeditah.
Vyhasanam kennaa praaptam kasya saukhyam nirantaram.

Whose life is perfect all the time? The answer is—no one's. Everyone has to accept their share of difficulties, be it defeat, disease or death. There is no manual for handling grief. It's a unique journey for each individual. A family can absorb shock much better as a unit. This is common sense, and when it is understood and accepted in its entirety, it becomes wisdom.

Once, Gautama Buddha was approached by a woman who had lost her son due to snakebite. She was told that Buddha was the only one who could bring him back to life. Buddha understood her predicament and, knowing well that it was not possible to bring her son back to life, asked her to sit down. He told her that he would revive her son if she could get a pinch of salt for him, not from her own home but from any home in town. She was very happy and got up to rush to get a pinch of salt which she thought would be very easy. As she got up, Buddha said, 'Please get salt only from a home where there has never been any bereavement.' She left quickly and Buddha waited for her to come back. Late at night, she returned and Buddha asked her to give him the pinch of salt. She told him, 'Oh Lord! There was no home where there was no bereavement, and therefore, I could not get even one pinch of salt.' She had understood that bereavement was a universal phenomenon.

'There is nothing on this earth more to be prized than true friendship.'

—*Thomas Aquinas*

Picking up the Right Friends

Chanakya gives a deep insight regarding the importance of friendship and choosing the right people as your close friends.

1. **Best Friend**

Vidhya mitram pravaaseshu bhaaryaa mitram grahesh cha.
Vyaadhitasyaushadham mitram dharmo mitram mritasya cha.

Chanakya said that once you are away from home and
your comfort zone, you can rely only on your skills and
knowledge, as you know nobody in that foreign land.
Therefore, be prepared to face a new set of people and
become self-reliant. At home, your partner is your best
friend with whom you can share your success as well as
difficulties, and vice versa. Remember, a spouse is always
a pillar of strength, which is why mutual respect, trust
and faith are important. For a patient, his best friend is
the right doctor. Chanakya also said that your dharma is
your best friend after death.

In the age of globalization, moving to foreign lands has
become common. In the initial phase of settling down,
everyone has to rely on their skills; one should learn
about the new setup, culture, and rules and regulations,
so that adapting to and docking into a new place becomes
easier and less troublesome. In the absence of joint or
close-knit families, it becomes all the more important to
share problems with partners. Avoid fixating on yourself
and learn to share the basics, such as earnings, property
and savings with your partner. Why keep problems to

yourselves? What is the idea of a family if the members cannot share everything with each other—good or bad?

2. **A Wicked Friend Is the Worst Thing That Can Happen to You**
Durjaneshu cha sarpeshu varam sarpo na durjanah.
Sarpo dashaati kaalen durjanastu pade-pade.
According to Chanakya, a venomous snake is less evil than a wicked friend. This is because a snake bites only once, whereas a cunning friend will sting you again and again, as long as you are his friend. Therefore, one must be clear about the integrity of a friend. My experience tells me that sometimes the best of friends can betray you and you may be surprised how much they can hurt you, not only emotionally, but financially as well. Therefore, as a corollary, never share everything with even the closest friend and never make a friend a partner in your business. In business, if a friend cheats you, you will lose your business as well as your friend. Same goes with relatives; never do business with relatives as it can land you in serious trouble. When it comes to sharing, be it emotions or support, families should be the mainstay, but a family business has a high chance of failure and dispute.

3. **Dealing with Friends**

Arendumvalmbya kunjjaar na kopyet.

If you deal with people or friends who are powerful, then never ever invite their wrath. In simple words, avoid confrontation, because in their rage, they can destroy you, especially if they are more capable than you. One must observe the way the mafia and underworld operates— they always keep powerful friends and enemies at arm's length. If there is a dispute, the one who is weak bows out gracefully, avoiding unnecessary bloodshed. Same goes with national security and international relations. You cannot upset or fight with a powerful neighbouring country. One has to be on the side of the nations with an economic or military clout.

Similarly, a weak ally is of no use. During World War II, Germany under Hitler could forge an alliance only with Japan, Italy and Spain (limited role and support). Except Japan, the other two were hardly of any use, economically or militarily.

4. **Part Gracefully and Without Remorse**

Ekvrikshe samaaroodhaa naanaavarnavihangamaah.
Prabhaae dikshu gaachahathi tara ka parvedanaa.

While we expect relationships and friendships to last

forever, it doesn't happen always. Even the best of relationships can be transient, for various reasons. The way to part should be graceful and without any ill feelings. I always told my students that once you quit a job, do it with grace and resolve it amicably with decent dialogue. Never leave with a bad taste in your mouth. In the professional world, bad news travels faster than good, and you pay a heavy price for an action that could have very well been avoided. At the same time, there should be no remorse once a friendship is broken or if one loses a job. According to this sutra, there are hundreds of different birds sleeping on a tree. In the morning, they go in different directions and also to different destinations; there is nothing to feel bad about it. When children grow up, they settle down with their spouses and start their own family. Often, parents are left with an 'empty nest'. They do feel the absence of their children; after all, they stayed with them for a long time. But parents have to move on. Those parents who cannot cut the proverbial umbilical cord and still interfere in the affairs of their children once they grow up can spell trouble for the family. Although it is difficult to digest, it is wise to move on.

Self-preservation

1. **There Is No Progress Without Wisdom**
   Antasarvihinannamupdesho na jayate.
   Malyachal sansaprana venushchanddanayatey.
   You can improve only if you are willing to learn from others. An unwise person will not be able to understand and absorb whatever is being taught to him through practical or theoretical means. Chanakya said that there is no point in giving sermons to someone who is devoid of wisdom, because they will all go to waste. He gave a simple example to illustrate his point by saying that a bamboo tree cannot become a sandalwood tree even if it is grown in the middle of a huge jungle of sandalwood trees.
   It is common knowledge that people who are not ready to listen or are dumb-witted will never be able to understand what is being told to them.

2. **Importance of Self**
   Tyajedakam kulasyaarthe graamassyaarthe kulam tyajet.
   Graamaam janapadasyaarthe aattmaarthe prithiveem tyajat.
   Self-protection and self-preservation are important, but so is the preservation of your conscience and your beliefs. If you disappear from this earth or your conscience

evaporates, then the existence of other things doesn't really matter.

Chanakya added that you can sacrifice a person for the sake of a family, a family for a village, and a village for the state, but for self-preservation and existence, the entire world can be sacrificed. Here, one has to look at the larger picture and the larger good. Remember, Chanakya was an advisor to the kings and hence, such harsh advice was very practical. As the head of an organization and as a leader, you must always look at the larger good and take decisions accordingly.

It is no surprise then that the US government has a huge underground bomb-proof shelter where the US president, top government and military staff can be safely housed if there is a devastating nuclear attack on America. It is a small, self-contained underground city with all facilities, to house around 1,500 people. This is to ensure that even if there is a catastrophe, the government can still run to bring America back on its feet!

Practical Advice

Chanakya laid emphasis on always being ready for any eventuality as an individual or as the head of an organization.

Anticipation and forward thinking are the keys to success. He also gives a tip that one should never look for perfection because nothing in nature is perfect. As long as the work is done, one shouldn't find faults just for the sake of it.

1. **Anticipation and Preparedness**

Anaagat vidhaataa cha prattutpannamatistathaa.
Dvaavetau sukhameveta yaddbhavishyo vinashyati.

Far-sightedness is the keys to success, and preparedness and planning, the key to victory. I believe that anticipation is an important habit we must cultivate. For a Formula One racing driver, handling the clutch, the brake, the accelerator, the gears and the steering wheel are important; but, the most important for him is 'anticipation', that is, to keep a track of who is coming from the left, which driver is rash, the next tunnel, where he can find a gap to overtake others and where the next difficult curve on the track is—these are the important aspects that would decide the winner. I always tell management students to keep an eye on the rear-view mirror to anticipate which technology or idea is coming from the rear to overtake the present one, so that they can change gears quickly to counter it. A head of the organization or a CEO in a leadership role is not only paid for handling day-to-day affairs, but is also paid for thinking ahead so that he can anticipate how things would be unfolding in the future, and remain ready, financially as well as resourcefully, to counter any challenges that may come up in the future. Therefore, never be sluggish in your actions and remain on your toes; be prepared all the time and victory will always favour you.

2. **Nothing Is Perfect**

Gandham suvarne phlmikshudande.
Nakari pushpam kalu chandanasya.
Vidvan dhani bhoopatideerghajivi.
Dhatu puraa kiapina bhudhidoabhoot.

All creations have shortcomings. Good authors should concentrate on the essence of their story, and not flowery language. They should worry about whether the whole piece makes sense, effectively conveys what they want to convey, and has the potential to create the desired impact. Similarly, many actors look for perfection, yet some great actors are spontaneous and look at the overall effect of the performance in a shot, not bothering about the minute details like whether the collar of the shirt was ironed or not or one eyebrow was not properly done.

Chanakya expressed this by saying that gold shines but

has no smell, sandalwood has fragrance but no flowers, sugarcane has no fruit, a scholar is not wealthy and seldom wealthy kings have a long life.

The idea—imperfect is perfect—is perfect, because the idea itself is imperfect.

A story in this context will be in order:

There was a valiant fighter who had a beautiful strong horse who was his companion in all battles. After winning several battles, he returned to the kingdom and as people gathered around him, he patted the horse and said, 'This is the best horse in the world'. Every one clapped till a silly guy went up to the horse, lifted his tail and sniffed his arse and said, 'Oh your horse stinks!'

'Use what you possess since the woods would be very silent if no birds sang there except those who sang the best.'

—*Henry Van Dyke*

In a Nutshell: Wisdom and Common Sense

1. **Similarities:** Most of the philosophical statements have been accepted over centuries across the world because they are simple and appealing to all. They are short, pithy and can be applied to daily life. Wisdom and common sense are similar as they are simple, effective and practical.

2. **Karma and Actions:** We are responsible for our own actions. Be prepared for the consequences of your actions as the consequences will never spare you.

3. **Values and Moksha:** Truth is the most important entity. One should remain truthful and abide by the rules of dharma. Suffering and death are great levellers. When you go to a burial ground, you realize that the material things you have been running after actually mean nothing.

4. **Family:** Family is very important. Bring up your children with care. Educate them. A worthy son is a priceless asset and a good-for-nothing son is a burden on the whole family.

5. **Individuality:** Siblings may have different traits; you should treat each one equally and not differentiate.

6. **Grief is Universal:** Loss of a family member can be devastating, but you must understand that this is inevitable. Learn how to move on.

7. **Picking Up the Right Friends:** Select your friends carefully. They should be dependable and forthcoming when you need them.

8. **Beware of Wicked Friends**: A snake may bite you once, but a friend can bite you again and again. Always end a friendship in an amicable way.

9. **Self-preservation:** Preserve your existence and your conscience. If you are dead and gone, nothing else matters.

10. **Importance of Wisdom:** Survival deems it necessary that you acquire knowledge and wisdom.

11. **Practical Advice:** One must do his/her job well, even though one cannot always be perfect. Being a perfectionist or wanting to be one can make your as well as the life of your subordinates difficult. Instead, anticipate problems so that nothing can wreck your plans.

7

SAAM DAAM DAND BHED

*'Diplomacy is the art of letting
someone else have your way.'*

—Daniele Varo

Everybody, be it a leader, a king, head of a state, general, diplomat, bureaucrat or an ordinary individual, faces difficult situations. We also come across people who create these situations regularly and who must be handled properly so that such a situation is resolved—come what may. If a favourable outcome cannot be brought about, it can cause embarrassment as well as loss of wealth and property for nations, organizations and even individuals. The key is, 'come what may, you have to find a solution to the problem'; therefore, one way or the other, one needs to address the problem at hand and resolve it, using all possible means, strategies and tactics at his or her disposal.

Chanakya proposed a four-pronged strategy to address any tricky situation, problem or person. Use it according to the situation and, if necessary, use more than one strategy at the same time.

I. Saam (Dialogue): The first approach uses dialogue; it is an effective way that also requires the least amount of money, resources or efforts. Territorial disputes or immigration, illegal migrations, extraditions, treaties, handling the interests of the diaspora and difference of opinion on some critical global issues can be handled efficiently with dialogue. In this scenario, one tries all persuasive methods to convince the other party that an amicable solution would be beneficial to both the sides. Both the parties need to have an open mind and should be willing to find a win-win solution. However, if one of the parties becomes greedy or rigid, this would fail.

The World Wars were fought when all dialogue failed. That is why it is said that one should never completely abandon talks—keep the communication channels open till the last moment. As national interest is of paramount importance for a nation, organizational interest is important for a company and its management. At a personal level, your interest becomes the sole purpose for you as an individual.

There are different ways to initiate a dialogue with the adversary:

1. **Praise:** The best way is to praise the other person so that his ego is boosted. You can say that you appreciate his pedigree, achievements, maturity and educational background.

2. **Social Network:** Bring up his or her old associations and linkages like being from the same neighbourhood, same clan or same school. In case of Pakistan, India has tried people-to-people dialogue and asserted that we are, after all, the same people, with a similar culture, food, dress and language.

3. **Mutual Benefit:** One can also point out mutual benefits that would accrue if a solution is found.

4. **Incentive:** If there is internal unrest, where different political and non-state actors are creating a problem for the state, one can give some recognition or award to tame the warring group of people.

An Illustration of Diplomatic Effort through Dialogue between India and Pakistan

In case of India and Pakistan, the two neighbouring countries, there have been continuous efforts to resolve issues through dialogue. Yet, there were two major wars and a Kargil operation between them. The bone of contention has been Kashmir and, of course, the liberation and creation of Bangladesh. Since both the nations have nuclear weapons, an all-out war has been ruled out; a dialogue with a sensible give-and-take arrangement would be the only answer to this complex situation. However, here the situation is more complex because of Pakistan's offensive posture as they promote terrorism as an extension of their war. Thus, in this case, a dialogue might not be the way forward for a peaceful outcome. Pakistan should understand that their own economy is in shambles and they have a debt of billions of dollars; in such a scenario, a peaceful coexistence between India and Pakistan would be good for the citizens of both the nations. But, when you make it a prestige issue, like Pakistan has made it out to be, a dialogue cannot resolve it. In this method of solution by dialogue, the most important thing is to identify whom to speak to and who is the decision-maker. India finds it difficult to deal with the Pakistani government because the elected government is controlled by their army, which is still sulking and licking their wounds inflicted during the two major wars.

Large corporations that face attrition on a large scale, go for a 'no-poaching agreement' whereby two or more of them sign an agreement that they would never poach talent from each other. This works in the BPO industry, media houses and telecom as well as pharmaceutical companies. This was possible only because they realized that it was affecting all of them and an amicable solution was found with the help of dialogue at the top management level.

At a personal level as well, dialogue is the answer to a conflict in relationships. You must know of families where siblings or even couples don't talk to each other because of misunderstandings. The best way is to initiate a dialogue. While 'who will call first' can become a big issue due to ego and emotions involved, a mature person, to break the deadlock, would simply pick up the phone, call and set up a meeting to iron out the differences. Most of the times, people break relationships for very trivial issues. These can be resolved by mature people through a meaningful dialogue. In close relationships, acknowledging one's mistakes and even saying 'sorry' helps break barriers.

II. Daam (Bribe): If dialogue doesn't work, then the next best way is to bribe your adversary by giving gifts, money or some materialistic comfort. For instance, the government of India has tried to pacify the people of Kashmir by granting special funds, special status and educational facilities so that people can join the mainstream. History is also full of many examples when a weaker kingdom has paid huge sums to the high and mighty to buy peace and security. The British did that with many small kingdoms in India—they asked them to pledge allegiance to the crown by paying them some money to retain their sovereignty.

Large corporations also go for some kind of compromise with competitors in the same geographical location and shed their market share to gain in some other areas. Family dispute between brothers can be resolved by dividing the ancestral inheritance in a sensible way to buy peace in the family.

The Kashmir dispute has seen this on several occasions—trade links were established so that the economy of Pakistan could benefit and 93,000 Pakistani prisoners of war were released in the hope of peace, but nothing worked.

III. Dand (Punishment): This is a strategy of applying force and punishing the enemy. However, invasion (attacking and conquering the enemy land, acquiring its resources and wealth and destroying him completely), in case of two countries, should always be the last resort. In Syria, and many other countries in the Middle East, Western powers are jointly attacking the ISIS and other terror groups. During the 1971 war between India and Pakistan, Indian forces joined hands with the Mukti Bahini in support of East Pakistan (now

Bangladesh) to liberate it physically from the clutches of West Pakistan, which was dominating and controlling it.

During World War II, after the collapse of Germany, the Allied Forces asked the Japanese to surrender or face the consequences of a nuclear strike several times. However, Japan was not prepared to surrender. Also, during that time, no one knew how powerful a nuclear explosion could be, and its capability for damage. When all negotiations failed, the United States had to detonate two bombs which ultimately lead to Japan's surrender. Thus, a severe punishment was unleashed on the Japanese to finally bring the war to an end.

People go to courts for property disputes and when nothing is forthcoming, some of them try pressure tactics and arm-twisting. They hire goons or the local mafia to help resolve the issue. The mafia actually thrives on 'dand' and are ready to smother your enemy for a price, which people gladly pay. Blackmail or psychological warfare are also employed to that end.

In recent times, 'dand' and 'daam' has been combined in a new methodology to punish adversary nations, known as 'economic sanctions'. Trade embargoes and defence deals are cancelled to put pressure on nations which do not fall in line.

IV. Bhed (Misunderstanding or planting a rift): Bhed means creating misunderstanding within your enemy group. You create differences within the enemy group and its decision makers, like sowing seeds of dissention. Man is the meanest and cleverest animal in the world and he has been using this strategy since the beginning of time. The Mahabharata is full of such deceit and debauchery.

The British used the divide and rule policy in India—they divided the kings of small provinces and drove them against each other so that they could rule such a large country with ease. Similarly, the Mughals had also used a similar strategy of pitching one king against the other. This can work well at a personal level as well.

There are several lessons to be learnt from this formula of divide and rule, which creates a rift in the enemy quarters, and the following points must be kept in mind at a strategic as well personal level:

1. Do not let your enemy join hands with anyone else; otherwise he will become strong. Enemy of your enemy is a friend, but a friend of your enemy also becomes your enemy, so, always keep them apart. Chanakya also tells us the ways of planting disinformation. Mostly wrong or misleading information is planted

by means of agents and double agents by nations.

2. In families, one may pose in such a way that siblings will start doubting each others' intentions. There is nothing on ground, but the whole thing is orchestrated in such a manner that blood relations start doubting each other and that is the beginning of the end of the family. To counter these, the first method, that is of dialogue, can work well. If you have doubts about your brother (planted in your mind by someone), then it can save you a fortune if you walk up to him and clarify any misinformation or misunderstanding. Most people don't do this and end up losing everything.

3. Never leave alone those who are jealous of you. They must be kept busy, else they could gang up and scheme against you. Preemptive action can save you from destruction.

Mind Games and Espionage

Dealing with your adversary is like playing a game of chess. It would be very easy to defeat your opponent in a game of chess if you could get to know what his next move would be or what his plan and strategy against you is. During the Cold

War period, billions of dollars were spent by the Russians and the Americans to build a spy network to read each other's mind. This espionage era had moles and counter moles and agents and double agents. These were carefully planted into government departments and some other sensitive organizations at high levels.

Each one knew that this game was being played and it was a case of 'I know that you know that I know'. Thus, there were times when the Russians knew that the Americans knew what the Russians were planning. Therefore, one had intelligence, counter-intelligence and counter-counter-intelligence to counter the counter-intelligence! The same happens in politics—you should know what your opponent is up to. In mafia gangs also, moles are planted to get information on the other gang.

In corporate life, it so happens that the boss is curious to know if you know his salary. It may also happen that the boss knows that you know that the boss knows that you know his salary! It's a mug's game.

The fact that your opponent knows that you know that he knows that you know is enough for him to be on his toes and feel insecure.

'Divide and rule, the politician cries; unite and lead,
is watchword of the wise.'

—*Johann Wolfgang von Goethe*

Business Intelligence and Competitive Intelligence

Business intelligence can be used by enterprises to support a wide range of business-related decisions ranging from operational to tactical to strategic. Basic operating decisions include product positioning or pricing. Strategic business decisions involve priorities, goals and directions at the broadest level. In all cases, it becomes most effective when it combines the data derived from the market in which a company operates (external data) with the data from the company's internal sources, such as financial and operational (internal data). When put together, the external and internal data can give a complete picture, which provides 'intelligence' that is very useful to handle the competition and improve your own performance.

Business intelligence is sometimes a synonym for competitive intelligence. Business intelligence uses technologies, processes and applications to analyse mostly internal data, structured data and business processes, while competitive intelligence gathers, analyses and disseminates information with a focus on company competitors. If understood broadly, business intelligence is the subset of competitive intelligence.

Chanakya was a very shrewd person, hence, his advice was lapped up by rulers and kings to their great benefit. There are some subtle sayings which can be interpreted and distilled to deliver brilliant ideas:

1. Never Hate Your Enemy

It sounds simple, but is not so easy to follow. When you curse your enemy, your own blood boils and it harms you physically, medically and psychologically. Hurt for hurt, an eye for an eye, a brick for a brick—this kind of thinking has been in existence since recorded history. But, do these things work? No, they don't.

The most damaging part is that anger gives you pain as long as it stays with you. It is like poison—the earlier you get it out of your system, the better it is. Another reason for not hating your enemy is conveyed brilliantly in the movie *Godfather III* where Michael Corleone, the don played by Al Pacino, tells his nephew, 'Don't hate your enemy; it will cloud your judgement.' When you are very angry and full of hatred, you do not think clearly. You are unable to take a proper decision to hit out at the enemy in the most optimized and telling manner.

As a corollary, whenever you get into a business or a job, you will have competition. It is prudent to know the strengths and weaknesses of your adversaries, but one should never have a fight with them.

'A rattlesnake, if cornered, will become so angry that it will bite itself. That is exactly what the harbouring of hate and resentment against others is—a biting of oneself. We think we are harming others in holding these spites and hates, but the deeper harm is to ourselves.'

—*E. Stanley Jones*

---

2. **Evil Days or Bad Times Distort Your Thought Process**

Na nirmitaa ken na drishtpoorvaa na shrooyate hemamayi kurangee.

Tathaapi trishnaa raghunandanassya vinaasha kaale vipreeta buddhih.

This is one of the most used quotes or expressions in today's times because it is so apt and true. '*Vinaasha kaale vipreeta buddhih*' means that when your bad time comes, you start thinking in the most illogical, irrational way, as if you are in a self-destruct mode. All your decisions go wrong and you are bound to get doomed. You refuse to listen to others and are not ready to take anyone else's advice.

Chanakya gave the example of Lord Ram who was asked by Sita to get her a golden deer she had seen in the jungle. Actually, the golden deer was a demon in disguise who was asked by Ravan to trick Ram and Laxman so that Ravan could avenge the injustice meted out to his sister Shurpanakha. Ravan wanted Ram and Laxman to move away from their ashram, leaving Sita alone so that he could kidnap her and take her away to Lanka, his kingdom.

Ram left Laxman behind to protect Sita, and chased the deer, finally killing it. The dying demon shouted, 'Oh Sita, oh Laxman, please help me', mimicking the voice of Ram. Sita got tricked and asked Laxman to go and help Ram. As soon as Laxman left Sita in her cottage, Ravan came in the guise of a sadhu and kidnapped Sita, taking her away to Lanka. In a nutshell, Ram, Laxman and Sita were destined for hardships and, hence, all three took the wrong decisions.

'If something has to go wrong, it will go wrong.'

—*Murphy's Law*

During World War II, when Germany was winning on all fronts, Hitler wanted to break the peace treaty and wage war against Russia, thus opening a new front. His generals advised him against it, as Russia was too mighty and the German army was already facing a shortage of manpower and equipment. It was also well-known that Russian winters are terrible and soldiers would find it impossible to sustain themselves in that weather. Hitler discarded all advice and ordered the invasion of Russia. This was the beginning of the end for Germany and eventually, they lost the war. This had to happen. The times went against Germany and Hitler's logic got distorted, eventually making the nation pay a heavy price.

While using the principle of 'Saam, Daam, Dand, Bhed', one must be cautious and weigh all the pros and cons. Be prudent and discuss them with your advisors thoroughly;

only then take a call to avoid an adverse situation. However, there is a dichotomy between decision-making and strategic thinking in the '*vinaasha kaale vipreeta buddhih*' hypothesis.

3. **Learn the Tricks of the Trade**

Doosadhyaampee susadhyan karotyapayagya.

He who knows the tricks of the trade makes even difficult jobs easy. Chanakya implied that one must be street-smart and thorough in his profession so that he is never lacking in terms of expertise. If one is armed with knowledge, experience and all that is required to handle a difficult situation, has a much higher chance of success than others. Therefore, education, training and practical experience all go hand in hand to winner.

4. **Be Unpredictable**

While tackling people and problems, your behaviour should not follow a typical pattern. If your actions and the way you think can be predicted by your adversary, he will always be in a position to counter you, as you have given him a chance to get prepared. The excitement in life is its uncertainty. A cricket match or a round of golf keeps you engaged because these games have unpredictable outcomes. To have an upper hand over others, unpredictability is the key. People should not be able to judge you or fathom your next move, unlike that of a machine. Do not repeat your behaviour and don't behave the same way in identical situations. Let others keep guessing. Don't be like Newton's law of motion— 'every action has an equal and opposite reaction'. Your opponents and even your subordinates should not know how you will react. People should not be able to say, 'I know exactly what he wants. He will not put any pressure beyond such a price. You handle others, and as far as he is concerned, I know how to handle him.'

Instead, people should say, 'While I can handle others, it is difficult to handle this guy because it is impossible to read his mind.'

One of the ways Hitler survived several assassination attempts was because he never followed a strict schedule; he would take a U-turn suddenly, leaving every one surprised. Most of the times, he changed his plans abruptly between meetings or events.

Just like a game of poker or bridge, it is all about keeping your moves a secret. This trait not only helps in negotiations and handling people in different situations, but also in increasing your bargaining power.

The flip side of the coin is that you should never go for a meeting with preconceived notions and being sure of the behaviour of your opponent. You should be prepared for the surprises he might throw at you!

The higher you go in stature, the more important it is to be a bit unpredictable with your actions, reactions and responses. In diplomacy, this plays a huge role. At the end of a meeting, both the sides should have some pluses and some minuses in their bags.

'Prepare for the unknown by studying how others in the past have coped with the unforeseeable and the unpredictable.'

—*George S. Patton*

In a Nutshell: Saam Daam Dand Bhed

1. **All of Us Face Difficult Situations**: All of us—a head of a state, a CEO or an ordinary man—come across difficult situations as well as difficult people who create problems for us.

2. **Need to Address Such Situations**: One has to handle such problems and find solutions before these go out of hand and snowball. These problems need to be solved immediately, and at any cost. There are four ways of addressing a problem, as per Chanakya.

3. **Saam**: Of the four ways to resolve a difficult situation, the first is through dialogue. Sit across the table and iron out your differences. Use all the persuasive methods to convince the other party that an amicable solution would be beneficial to both the sides. Here, both the parties need to have an open mind and should be willing to find a solution.

4. **Daam**: Use bribe when dialogue doesn't work. You can give gifts, money or some item of materialistic comforts to your adversary. History is full of many examples when a weaker kingdom has paid huge sums to the high and mighty to buy peace and security. These could be trade-offs which involve materialistic things.

5. **Dand**: Applying force and punishing the enemy is a last resort that nations use. Since this is a high-risk method, avoid it as far as possible. People go to court for resolving property disputes, and when nothing is forthcoming, some of them try pressure tactics and arm-twisting. They hire goons or the local mafia to help resolve the issue.

You can also punish your enemy in several different ways, such as through psychological warfare.

6. **Bhed**: Create differences within the enemy and its decision makers by sowing seeds of dissention. The Mahabharata is full of examples of this tactic. This can work well at a personal level as well.

7. **Practical Diplomacy Tips**: Know the strengths and weaknesses of your adversary, but never have a fight with them. Dealing with your adversary is like playing a game of chess. It would be very easy to defeat your opponent if you knew their next move or their plans and strategy against you.

8. **Learn the Tricks of the Trade:** He who knows the tricks of the trade makes even difficult jobs easy. One must be street-smart and thorough in his profession so that one is never lacking in terms of expertise.

8

ROLE OF DESTINY IN SUCCESS

'Name the greatest of inventors—accident.'

—Mark Twain

While doing my research, I asked this simple question—What, according to you, is the role of luck in your success on a scale of 1–10?—to more than three dozen successful people, from managers to businessmen to artists. To my surprise, the answers ranged from 3 to 10. Some responded that luck had played a little part in their success, while some went to the other extreme and responded that they believed luck was a very strong factor in their success. Entrepreneurs, businessmen, actors and singers respected luck a lot more than those with secure jobs.

In some professions, luck is more critical. For instance, people who have almost a linear path to follow do not depend on luck as such. Getting educated, entering the job market and working hard are bound to give good results. But, for start-ups, the case is different, as entering an unchartered business territory and eventually making profit cannot only depend on hard work and merit. Other factors outside of your control, internal as well as external, are also at play. Luck does play an important part and this really can't be brushed under the carpet.

When Sunil Mittal, the chairman of Bharati group, had to shut down his business of importing and marketing generator sets due to a policy change of the government, it was a case of pure bad luck. At the same time, the new telecom policy allowing privatization of telecom services was a Godsend opportunity—to counter his bad luck. Whether he got pushed into it or he pushed himself into it is irrelevant. The rest, as they say, is history; he spun out a multibillion dollar business and became one of the largest telecom operators. Hard work alone did not take him forward—god's hand or luck also played a part in it. As they say, 'Nothing succeeds like success.'

In case of showbiz, luck matters even more. Kishore Kumar and Rajesh Khanna's first collaboration, for instance, was a matter of luck. Kishore was a veteran singer but he actually shot to fame after he gave his voice to Rajesh Khanna. With R.D. Burman as the music director, the trio created pure magic at the box office. *Aradhana* is still considered one of the best movies of its time. As a blockbuster, it collected a whopping ₹17 crore at the box office in 1969, which was a huge sum then. Another factor in favour of Khanna was that romantic films were the order of the day in the early 1970s. The rebellious '80s saw the rise of the angry young man. This was the entry point of Amitabh Bachchan. Timing, place and people are all related to luck. As they say, '*Waqt se pehle aur mukkadar se zyada kuch nahin milta*' (You will not get anything before it's your time, and how much you will get is also decided by your destiny). Show business depends on the reaction of the audience. Sometimes a brilliant movie fails and an average one does great business at the box office. The director and the producers have yet to come out with a success formula. That is why most of them go to temples before their movies release. Many of them wear rings and stones prescribed by astrologers and pundits—all to woo lady luck!

'Captaincy is 90 per cent luck and 10 per cent skill. But, don't try it without that 10 per cent.'

—*Richie Benaud*

Contrary to popular imagination, luck is not only important in professional success but in every sphere of our life. Luck is how opportunities pop up or how great plans fall apart right in front of our eyes. Luck is about timing, and about how certain powers influence the outcome of your efforts. The risk factor is also based on luck; 'calculated risk' itself means the influence of outside factors which are beyond your control. You can calculate only to an extent and not more. If there was no luck factor, then there would have been no words like luck, destiny, god, almighty and, above all, faith.

'Faith begins where
Reason sinks exhausted.'

—*Albert Pike*

Let me narrate a short story:

There was a man who was unemployed because his company had folded due to financial crisis. He was desperately looking for a job, but despite his brilliant track record, qualifications and a positive attitude, he could not get it. One day, when he was driving back from the airport, dejected, with hardly a few dollars in his pocket, he saw a car parked on the other side of the road. An old couple was desperately waving for help. He stopped his car and asked the old man what had happened. He was told that their car had broken down and they had an urgent flight to catch. 'I have an important meeting to attend,' said the old man. 'Can you please fetch a cab, because the airport is almost 30 miles from here?'

This unemployed man, himself in a bad financial state, felt that he should do something for the old couple. He said, 'Come on, I will drop you. Let us load the luggage in my car's boot.' The old man was surprised and said, 'But, son, you are going the other way.' The man still helped them load their stuff and went back 30 miles to drop them at the airport. As he helped them get their luggage onto the trolley, the old man said, 'Here is my business card. I am back next week, do come and meet me.'

This man's jaw dropped as he looked at the card. The old man was the chairman and owner of one of the largest car manufacturers in the US. The next week, when he went to meet him, the chairman got up from his chair and said, 'What do you do for a living, son?' When he told the old man that he was unemployed and looking for a job, the old main said, 'Why don't you join me?' He was hired by the company then and there!

Now, what was this if not good fortune? As they say, '*Na jane kiss bhes main baba mill jaye bhagwan re*' (You don't know in what avatar you may meet god himself).

'Luck affects everything. Let your hook always be cast; in the stream you least expect it there will be a fish.'

—*Ovid*

On the flip side, the fish, not expecting anyone to cast the hook, is unlucky because someone decided to cast it.

Factors like god, faith and destiny are very humbling, and even when you achieve success, always remember that there are these bigger forces at play. If you look back at your life, you will realize that several major turning points came at certain moments which shaped your destiny.

'It is hard to detect good luck—it looks so much like something you have earned.'

—*Frank Clark*

Chanakya had also opined on destiny and the power of the Lord in his own ways:

1. **The Power of God Does Not Dwell in Idols but in Feelings**

   Such profound philosophy was encapsulated in one sentence by Chanakya. Man tries to create an image of god by creating idols of clay stone or even gold, and conveys their power through stories; ultimately, they all invoke feelings of faith, assurance and something to depend on. How you perceive the almighty, without anyone having seen the him, is a matter of faith. This feeling gives you comfort and a sense of safety, security and well-being. People worship a stone idol and it is often said, '*Na mano to paththar, mano to Bhagwan*' (If you don't believe, it is a piece of stone, but if you do, then it is God).

2. **Individual Flaws and Deficiencies Are Caused by Destiny for Which External Circumstances Cannot Be Held Responsible**

   Patram naiv yava karreravit pe dosho vasantasyakim. Nollokaappyavalokayate yadi diva sooryasya kim dooshanam? Varshaa naiv patati chaatakmukhe meghasya kim dooshanam.

Yattpoorva vidhinaa lalaat likhitam tanmanaarjitu kahkshaah?

Chanakya said that if leaves do not sprout in kareel (a medicinal plant), it is not the fault of the plant or of the spring season. If an owl cannot see in daylight, it is not the fault of the sun. If raindrops do not fall in the mouth of the chatak (cuckoo bird that only drinks rainwater as it pours down), it is not the fault of the clouds. No one can alter your destiny.

Therefore, individual deficiencies and deformities are a matter of fate. Why someone is born blind or deaf is a matter of destiny and you cannot blame a blind or a deaf person for that. Why is someone born into a poor family and another one into a royal family? These are all matters of destiny and god's will.

The flip side is that great qualities are also a gift of destiny. People are born singers, athletes, painters, sculptors, actors, scholars, poets and writers—these people have that something in them which others don't. That is also destiny. Great speakers, they say, have the gift of the gab. Yes, one can learn to sing and excel in it, but you need a good voice. You can work hard and become a singer but to become a Kishore Kumar or a Sonu Nigam, you need a golden voice. Then, you have to work hard on that gift of god to become one of the best.

3. **Why Worry in Life When the Lord Is There to Take Care of You**

Kaa chintaa mam jeevane yadi harivishvambharo geeyate.
No chedarbhakjeevanaarth jananeestannyam kuthum nihsaret.

Ittyaalochaya muhurmuhuryadu pate laxmipate kevalam.
Tvattapaadaambujsevanen satatam kaalo mayaa neeyate.

Chanakya reiterated that god is there to take care of all of us, as he loves all those who he has created. Had it not been for god, how does a mother's breasts fill with milk automatically for her child? Chanakya was trying to say that He who gives life also provides for its sustenance. He then stated that since nature is so vast and complex, it is better and wise to surrender to the lord and let Him take care of you.

4. **Basic Parameters of Human Life Are Formulated When the Human Being Is in the Embryonic Form**

Ayuh Karma Vittancha Viddyaa Nidhanmeva cha.
Paanchtani hi Srijjyante Garbhasthasyaiv Dehinah.

Your lifespan, profession, financial status, education and opportunities are all predetermined when you are in the womb.

Despite so much advancement in science and technology, we don't know where we came from and when and where we will die. In between these is what we call the journey of life, and even that is predetermined by the Lord. If one understands the enormity of this, their ego will get dissolved.

5. **It Is Your Fate That Can Make You Rich or Poor**
Ranka karoti raajaanam rajaanam rankamev cha.
Dhaninam nirdhanam chaiv nirdhanam dhaninam vidhih.
Chanakya gave yet another twist of wisdom by stating that it is one's fate that makes a beggar a king and a king a beggar. In the Bhagavad Gita, Krishna also said, '*Karam kar, 'phal ki asha mat kar'*, which means, keep doing your work and don't worry about the results. This is because your karam might be in your hands, but not the result.

At the time when India was about to get its freedom from the British, my parents lived in Lahore, which is now in Pakistan. As the idea of independence gathered momentum, so did the idea of dividing the country into two separate nations. My parents and their entire joint family were doing very well financially and had several factories and shops. They were living like kings.

Lahore was to come to India, and Calcutta (now Kolkata)

was to go to East Pakistan as per the discussions within the ruling class. My parents and grandparents wanted to stay in India and were happy that Lahore would be a part of India; thus, they did very little to move their belongings, cash or jewellery out of Lahore, even though the distance by road between Lahore and Amritsar is just 30 miles!

The decision to merge Lahore with West Pakistan came very late and there was no time for them to react. This was a twist of fate which changed everything overnight. They had to leave everything and move out of Lahore almost empty-handed. Now, what would you call this? Was anything else possible for them to do except to accept the wrath of god or destiny? I don't think there was anything they could do except save their own lives and reach Amritsar.

All the hard work of decades, the building of a business empire, and the peace of mind of the entire family was smashed by the fist of fate. The rich and mighty became paupers in one stroke of destiny.

6. **You Get Everything According to Your Destiny**
Tadrishee jayaytey budhivaryavsaayyoapi tadrishah.
Sahaayastadrishshash eva yadrishee bhavitavyataa.

Chanakya referred to destiny in several of his sutras. He gave a different perspective to the power and relevance of our destiny. Here, he was clear about the role of destiny and said that every action of ours as well as our reactions and responses are guided by our destiny. Destiny is supreme in our life; all things are predetermined. If you have to get something in life, then you will act or will be made to act in such a way that the results will be in your favour.

This reminds me of a famous song, 'Que sera, sera'. The lyrics of the song mean that whatever has to happen will happen. It implies that one should not worry about the future, indicating that everything is predestined. Here is the first stanza of the song:

When I was just a little girl
I asked my mother, 'What will I be?
Will I be pretty,
will I be rich?'
Here's what she said to me—

'Que sera, sera
Whatever will be, will be
The future's not ours to see
Que sera, sera
Whatever will be, will be.'

7. **You Come to This World All Alone and You Meet Your End Alone**

Janmamrittyurniyattyeko bhunakkttyetyekka shubhashubham.

Narkeshu patattyekah eko yati param gatim.

A man comes alone in this world and he alone has to bear the consequences of his deeds, good or bad. He has to suffer the torture of hell and also enjoy the fruits of heaven alone. Even though you live in a family, in a society or a cultural setting, you are all alone. Chanakya said that the bitter truth is that everything constantly changes and there is nothing that will exist forever. Your friends, companions, family—everything is transient. This understanding makes you face the world positively and fearlessly. Indirectly, it also tells us to remain detached from these worldly illusions because all this is bound to go one day. Detachment will make your departure easier.

Life is Full of Unpredictable Twists and Turns: An Illustration from a Real-Life Incident

Irrfan Khan, one of the finest actors in Indian cinema as well as in Hollywood, was diagnosed with a serious illness and was in England for treatment a while ago. The initial phase of treatment and his disease itself inflicted unbearable pain. He got diagnosed when he was at the peak of his career—now, that is destiny.

The actor chose to speak, in a rare interview with *The Times of India*, about the struggle, pain and fear he experienced after being diagnosed with neuroendocrine tumour.

But that was not the end. Pain was one of the biggest obstacles the actor faced. Khan said that there was a point when 'nothing was working'. The intensity of the pain was enormous. 'As if all this while, you were just getting to know pain, and now you know his nature and his intensity. Nothing was working; no consolation, no motivation. The entire cosmos becomes one at that moment—just pain, and pain felt more enormous than even God.'

The rarity of his condition made his situation all the more unpredictable. At one point in the interview, he said, 'I was a part of a trial-and-error game.'

The actor went on to add that he has since decided to 'submit, surrender and trust, irrespective of the outcome, irrespective of where this takes me, eight months from now, or four months from now, or two years. You are just a cork floating in the ocean with unpredictable currents,' admitted Khan, on battling this disease.

Did God Create Man or Did Man Create God?

An ongoing quest for mankind is to find peace and solace in this treacherous world. Where do we come from when we are born and where do we go after death—these are certain questions which we have not been able to figure out the answers to yet. That is why the idea of God Almighty emerged. There has to be a power or something that runs the universe, people thought. Therefore, we created an entity called the Almighty in our minds and assumed that He created us. Thus, was it God who created man or man who created God? This is a question that needs to be kept in mind. We wanted something to look up to, hang on to during a crisis in our lives and God, in whatever form we took him to be, became a source of solace. Then came godmen and gurus who took upon themselves the task of showing us a way out of our misery, interpreting the meaning of the Almighty. They also showed us the path to reach God. Thinkers—not godmen—like Chanakya, Aristotle, Plato and Socrates showed the philosophy of living, the meaning of life which was nothing but to make you see the reality of life.

Grandparents and even our parents who realized this through experiences as well as reading became mentors for their children. They were a part of a support system. But, with the advent of the nuclear family, this is disappearing rapidly from our day-to-day lives. Is the present generation of children missing something? Of course yes!

When we were kids, I remember our grandmother told us to shove the problem that was most troubling to us under the pillow at night and sleep over it. She assured us that we would get some solution in the morning. And most of the times, this worked!

If I sit back and think about it now, I would say, 'Though the problem didn't disappear overnight, in the morning there was a chance that we completely forgot about it or we would get some fresh ideas to solve it. In a nutshell, we would have slept well in the hope of a favourable outcome!'

I am saying this to show that there is no point losing your sleep to will problems. Leave it to God, and some solution may come your way. This is one way of pacifying yourself and moving on. It's another way of saying, 'Que sera, sera'.

'Never cut what you can untie.'

—*Joseph Joubert*

In a Nutshell: Role of Destiny in Success

1. **Need for Luck**: Luck is critical in some professions more than others. Entrepreneurs, businessmen, actors, singers, etc. need luck a lot more than those with secured jobs.

2. **Luck and Life**: If there was no luck factor, then there would have been no words like luck, destiny, God, Almighty and, above all, faith. Luck is not only important for professional success, but it plays a role in every sphere of our life.

3. **Worry:** God is in faith and not in idols. He is there to take care of us, therefore, there is no point in worrying.

4. **Skills**: Individual strengths and weaknesses are provided by destiny and that is why some are born deaf, some blind and some healthy. Being a great painter, actor, singer or a person with business acumen are gifts from god too.

5. **Wealth**: Fate makes us rich or poor. It is a matter of timing, the people you meet, where you are born and a few other external factors that shape your future and the path you are destined to take.

6. **Nothing Exists Forever**: A man comes to this world alone and meets his end alone. The bitter truth is that everything constantly changes and there is nothing that will exist

forever. Your friends, companions, family, everything is transient—this understanding makes you face the world positively and fearlessly.

9

INTELLECT AND EDUCATION

'Education is more than a luxury; it is a responsibility that society owes to itself.'

—Robin Cook

Can anyone become successful without knowledge, education and intellectual prowess? The answer is no. Intellect is the faculty of reasoning and understanding objectively, especially with regard to abstract matters. Knowledge is the possession the facts, information, and skills acquired through experience or education—the theoretical or practical understanding of a subject. Both these are acquired through worldly experience and formal education. Being an educationist, I always lay emphasis on formal education because it gets you ready to interact with the world in a more meaningful way. Education also augments your capacity to solve problems at work and be a more productive member of the society. All competitive exams are usually a test of knowledge and the ability to apply that knowledge to handle different situations.

All things considered, a well-read, knowledgeable person will have a better personality and much more confidence to handle problems than the one who isn't. Today, we live in the Knowledge Age, where acquiring knowledge has become easier than before, but interpreting it and understanding its application (which is related to your intellect) is a bigger challenge.

Centuries ago, Chanakya elaborated his ideas and thoughts on the value of education so well that they are relevant even today. In fact, his ideas are much more relevant than ever before. Here are some of his concepts on education which can be incorporated in our lives:

1. **Education Is like the Cow of Plenty—It Protects and Provides like a Mother**

   Kamadhenugunaa viddya hayakaale phaladaayani.
   Pravaase bhaatrisadrisha viddya guptam dhanam smritam.
   Chanakya said that education is like a cow which gives us milk even in our most difficult times. It is like a secret treasure and renders help anytime we need it.

People invest in gold, property and land so that it can appreciate in value; a property can also be rented out for an income. I always tell my students that you must first invest on yourself in terms of education so that you can reap the benefits throughout your life, and your value (in terms of net worth and salary) will keep compounding as you get more experience. Once you are well-placed in life, you will also get a partner of equal stature who would be earning as good as you and, thus, your income will be doubled! You can lose money, property or land but no one can steal your education and knowledge from you; therefore, education is the best investment.

2. **Since Education Helps to Get Everything, It Is Revered Everywhere and by Everyone**

   Viddvaan prashaste loke viddvaan sarvatra gauravam. Viddyayaa labhata sarva viddyaa sarvatra poojyate.

   A well-read person and an educated being would get praise and respect from every one; he also earns a good reputation in the society. Whatever one may think, one thing is clear that an educated person will always have an edge over the one who is uneducated. It is across the world and more so in developing economies. Education opens the door of opportunities and that is why millionaires as well as the poor send their children to study. A rich person wants an educated son or daughter to take his empire forward and a poor man wants his educated child to build a new empire.

Education is also a great leveller; it puts you on an equal platform with the high and mighty. For instance, if a person gets into the civil services because of his sound education, he may be able to get married to someone of his own stature. This is generally the norm, barring some exceptions.

3. **You Cannot Get Comfort and Education Simultaneously**
   Sukhaarthee chet tyejedviddyam viddyaarthee chet tyajettsukam.
   Sukhaartheenah kuto viddya kuto viddyaarthinah sukham.
   There is no gain without pain and that is also applicable to education. A student must be able to undertake some amount of sacrifice and accept a bit of discomfort if required, to get himself educated. To study well, one may have to give up the luxury of their home; sometimes, they may have to travel by bus every day to their school or college in the heat and dust. The college curriculum can be very demanding with assignments, projects and late-night discussions and may not even allow you to get

enough sleep. You may have to sacrifice holidays and be prepared to rough it out as and when required.

A well-rounded MBA programme is very taxing and two years are a gruelling experience, but after that, you get the wings to fly as high as you wish to. I, in my opening address to the new batch, would often narrate a dialogue from the film *Chak De! India* where Shah Rukh Khan says to the hockey team, '*Sattar minute hain tumhare pass. Yeh sattar minute tumhari zindagi ke saab se khaas sattar minute honge. Yeh sattar minute tumse koi nahin chheen sakta. Agar har player aaj sabse achchee hocky khel gaya to yeh sattar minute tumsey khuda bhi wapas nahin maang sakta. Yeh sattar minute tumhe zindagi bhar yaad rahenge—tum haaro ya jeeto. Toh aaj jao aur khelo, jitna achcha khel sakte ho, jee bhar kaar khelo.*' This roughly translates to, 'You have seventy minutes to play this game and these are the most important and special seventy minutes of your life. Nobody will be able to snatch away these seventy minutes from you, not even god. Whether you win or lose, these seventy minutes will remain with you throughout your life. So, give your best and play your best hockey with all your heart.'

This is exactly what is important for a student seeking knowledge. He has to do his best, sweat it out and not worry about his discomfort, heat and hurt in the formative years. He must bash on regardless.

'I'm not a teacher: only a fellow traveller of whom you asked the way. I pointed ahead—ahead of myself as well as you.'

—*George Bernard Shaw*

---

4. **Respect Your Guru to Get Knowledge**

Yathaa khanittvaa khanitren bhootale vaari vindati.
Tathaa gurugataam viddyaam shushrushuradhigachhati.

Just like you have to dig hard and deep into the ground to get water, you need to make all the effort to extract knowledge from your guru or your teacher. I have seen students who are very keen to learn and clarify their difficulties from the teacher and make the best of it. However, there are some who are casual and do not bother to clarify their doubts or shy away from going to the teacher if they need some additional inputs. I have also observed that students from engineering and management institutes, who are serious about learning, make all the effort to extract maximum information out of the experience of the faculty.

5. **An Uneducated Man Is a Pauper**

Dhanheeno na cha heenashcha dhanik sa sunishchayah.
Viddhya ratnen heeno yah sa heenah sarvavstushuh.

Chanakya said that a person who does not possess materialistic wealth is not a pauper as he will be able to earn later in life. But, a person without education is a real pauper because the years he lost not seeking education cannot come back. Therefore, invest in education from an early age.

6. **The Uneducated Are a Dead Load on Earth**

Yeshaam na viddya no tapo na daanam na chaapi sheelam na guno na dharamah.

Te mrittuloke bhuvi bhaarbhootaa manushyaroopen mrigaashcharanti.

Those who do not have manners, knowledge, determination and virtues are like deadwood and a burden on the society as well as on the planet. The productivity of a man is usually proportional to his skills, knowledge and other good traits and without all these he is a load on the society. If we see our own country, we have a young population with 65 per cent people below 35 years of age, yet most of them are not employable because they do not have any skills or knowledge to be absorbed in a job or to do something of their own. The Skill India initiative by the government is doing exactly that—trying to make people employable so that they can contribute to the society.

'He was so learned that he could name a horse in nine languages; so ignorant that he bought a cow to ride on.'

—*Benjamin Franklin*

---

7. **One Should Be Able to Pick up the Right Things from of the Vast Amount of Available Knowledge**
Anantashaastram bahilaashcha viddyya alpam dakaalo bhauvighnataa cha.
Aasabhootam tadupaasneeyam hanso yathaa ksheermivaambupaddhyaat.
Chanakya said that (according to mythology) as a swan can extract milk out of a mixture of water and milk, one should be able to extract the appropriate pieces of

knowledge from the vast reservoir of available knowledge. In the Information Age of today, one can get any kind of content from the internet, be it books, movies, songs, articles, opinions or news, at the push of a button. The most important thing to keep in mind is what to look for, how to use the right data and information, how to interpret it and then how to use it judiciously.

How to extract the right information from the vast resources available to us is an art. If one does not learn to do so, a person will waste his time and will not be able to get what is relevant for him. Nowadays, we suffer from 'information overload', that is, we have so much information that we find it difficult, if not impossible, to handle it.

Since the information is so easily available, students resort to cut, copy and paste. This is hugely damaging to our learning mechanism. I always insisted that my students submit handwritten assignments to ensure that blind copy-paste was not possible.

The best way to use the internet for learning is to get all the information that you require from it and then write it in your own words, using important data or facts that you have gathered.

I will go one step forward and say that even a college or

a school is like an ocean of knowledge and it depends on you what you make of it. It is like a bowl full of honey; a bee comes and takes 5 grams of honey, another one takes 50 grams, and yet another takes 200 grams. It depends on the individual bee how much it takes, as the bowl has more than enough to offer everyone.

8. **Move out of Your Home to Get Knowledge**
Grihaasaktassya no viddyaa na dayaa maansabhojinah.
Dravya lubdhassya sattyam na strainassya pavitrataa.
These words were crafted such a long time ago and are yet so profoundly true and relevant. Those who do not want to move out of their comfort zone, that is, their home or their town to get education can never get the best of it. It is important for the parents to understand that they should let their children move out for education. It is not possible to have all the colleges in the city you live in; therefore, let your children go out to the cities and even countries which provide specialized knowledge. This definitely adds to the cost of education but it will be worth the effort and money. Staying away from home itself is a learning experience because a young person has to learn to manage things on their own. It makes one more confident and independent.

I have also seen that parents are too bothered about the comfort of their children, even in hostels. Basic things are important but you cannot pamper your children to the extent that they do not learn to live like others. No special treatment should be sought for your children.

'A ship in harbour is safe—
but that is not what ships are built for.'

— *John A. Shedd*

---

9. **Discipline is the Bedrock of Learning**
Aalasyopahataa viddyaa parahastam gatam dhanam.
Alpabeejahatam kshetram hatam senyamanaayakam.
A lazy and undisciplined pupil will never be able to acquire knowledge because discipline and dedication are two of the most important attributes for learning and getting educated. Look at those who cracked various prestigious and difficult competitive exams, or got scholarships in foreign universities; they all had a few things in common—they worked very hard and were disciplined and methodical in their studies. They made a rigorous timetable for themselves and were able to sustain

this for the required period. They remained focused to achieve their target and forgot about sleep, entertainment and sometimes even food. To develop your intellect, you need to be disciplined in your life. And one must remember that learning doesn't stop, it's a lifelong process. Chanakya also talked about the control of money and personal fiscal discipline while handling finances. He said that those who do not control their money will lose it to others. In general, any aspect of life requires proper control. An army cannot win a battle without a commander and a field remains barren if it is not ploughed for years.

'Part of the American myth is that people who are handed the skin of a dead sheep at graduating time think that it will keep their minds alive forever.'

—*John Mason Brown*

---

10. **Learning From Other Creatures**

Singhodekam bakaadekam sikshechattvari kukkutaat.
Vaaysaatpanch shikshechshat shat shanstreeni gardabhaat.

Chanakya told us that one can learn a lot from animals and birds since they have special talents which one can intelligently emulate and replicate in their own life. He said that you can learn from a crow, a heron, a lion, a cock, a dog and even a donkey.

Whether you are big or small, you must do every task with full power and to your full capacity. A lion will never do anything half-heartedly; he kills a rabbit and attacks an elephant with the same ferocity and force. This approach guarantees success.

A heron has a tremendous capacity to remain focused and has a sense of concentration while going for its target. It has a great sense of timing and distance too. Herons primarily feed on small fish, but they are opportunistic feeders and will eat whatever comes within striking distance. They occasionally snack on shrimps, crabs, small mammals, amphibians, small birds, and even insects. If we remain focused and concentrate our energies to hit at our target, we will always succeed.

A cock can teach us four things—first, get up at the right time and that is the greatest asset of successful people. They start earlier than their competition. As they say, 'early bird catches the worm'. Second, fight bitterly with your might and this guarantees success as well. Third, make such a fierce attack that the enemy's entire flock runs away. Fourth, when you are fighting for something, don't protect only your own share but also grab the share of your opponent. So, start early, fight bitterly, make others run for their money and then, grab their territory.

A crow is no ordinary bird. For self-preservation, a crow copulates in a clandestine way. It collects useful things from time to time to add to his resources. It doesn't trust other birds and always remains alert. It makes a lot of noise when required to gather everyone around itself. These can be used by us very intelligently for our own survival.

A dog is man's best friend. A dog can enjoy and be satisfied even with something little given to him to eat. He is always alert, even in slumber. A dog is always faithful and stands by those who love him and will never abandon them. It is brave and can defend itself. Out of all these characteristics, I feel that being loyal to the people who are good to you is the most important trait that one can learn from a dog.

People look down upon a donkey and think it to be a useless animal with no brain. Yet, it has qualities which we can learn from. First, it has the capacity to carry heavy loads and manage it despite being very tired and exhausted. Second, it remains happy and keeps working even during the worst weather conditions.

Therefore, one can learn great lessons from animals and

birds around us as they have certain very strong traits

11. **Learn from Your Enemy**

Shatrorpi sugunyo graha.

Learning from your enemy or your adversary is a very old art which has been practised by emperors, kings, politicians, generals and heads of business organizations. First, one should never underestimate the enemy. Most people go wrong because of poor intelligence about the enemy and also overconfidence in their own abilities. Every adversary has certain good traits that one can learn from. During major military campaigns, it is not surprising that field commanders and generals maintain dossiers of their enemy counterpart. During World War II, German generals maintained details of temperament, tactics, strategic thinking, military acumen and personal habits of the generals from the Allied Forces pitted against them. You not only learn from the enemy, you can also anticipate his actions in advance.

The Dalai Lama once said, 'Your enemy is your greatest teacher.' In politics, two rival political parties learn a lot about tactics and strategies from each other during a political campaign. Does your enemy spend a lot on digital marketing or does he have massive rallies where senior leaders go and address the masses? How do they ensure that every target voter is addressed properly with a relevant message from the top leadership? How do they optimize spending their money and other resources? Therefore, keep a firm eye on the intentions and working methodology of your adversary and keep learning, sometimes countering and sometimes admiring what your enemy does.

'It would be possible to describe everything
scientifically, but it would make no sense;
it would be without meaning, as
if you described a Beethoven symphony as a
variation of wave pressure.'

—*Albert Einstein*

In a Nutshell: Intellect and Education

1. **Theory and Practice**: Knowledge is possessing facts, information and skills acquired through experience or education; the theoretical or practical understanding of a

subject. It is acquired through worldly experience as well as formal education.

2. **Personality Development:** Formal education gets you ready to interact with the world in a more meaningful way and also augments your capacity to solve problems at work and as a responsible member of the society. All things considered, a well-read and knowledgeable person will have a better personality and much more confidence to handle problems than the one who isn't.

3. **Education as an Investment:** Education is a great investment. It is like a cow that gives you milk even in your difficult days. Since it is so valuable, every one reveres education. One should strive to pick up the right things from the ocean of available knowledge.

4. **Comfort Zone:** You have to make efforts to get education. You have to move out of your comfort zone, that is, your home, if you want education. You must respect your teachers and extract the maximum out of them.

5. **Discipline:** Most importantly, you need to be disciplined throughout your learning days to make the best of it.